This is
Salvaged

ALSO BY VAUHINI VARA

The Immortal King Rao

This is
Salvaged

Vauhini Vara

Grove Press UK

First published in the United States of America in 2023 by
W. W. Norton & Company, Inc.

First published in Great Britain in 2024 by Grove Press UK,
an imprint of Grove Atlantic

1 3 5 7 9 8 6 4 2

A CIP record for this book is available from the British Library.

Trade paperback ISBN 978 1 80471 062 3
E-book ISBN 978 1 80471 063 0

Printed in Great Britain by TJ Books Ltd, Padstow, Cornwall

Grove Press UK
Ormond House
26–27 Boswell Street
London WC1N 3JZ

www.groveatlantic.com

For my sister,
Krishna Dweepa Vara

—in the end they'd made her laugh: Ha! Ha! Ha! Ha! Ha! Ha! Ha! Ha!
Ha! Ha! Ha! Ha! Ha! Ha! Ha! Ha! Ha! Ha! Ha! Ha! Ha! Ha! Ha! Ha! Ha!
Ha! Ha! Ha! Ha! Ha! Ha! Ha! Ha! Ha! Ha! Ha! Ha! Ha! Ha! Ha! Ha! Ha!
Ha! Ha! Ha! Ha! Ha! Ha! Ha! Ha! Ha! Ha! Ha! Ha! Ha! Ha! Ha! Ha! Ha!
Ha! Ha! Ha! Ha! Ha! Ha! Ha! Ha! Ha! Ha! Ha! Ha! Ha! Ha! Ha! Ha! Ha!
Ha! Ha! Ha! Ha! Ha! Ha! Ha! Ha! Ha! Ha! Ha! Ha! Ha! Ha! Ha! Ha! Ha!
Ha! Ha! Ha! Ha! Ha! Ha! Ha! Ha! Ha! Ha! Ha! Ha! Ha! Ha! Ha! Ha! Ha!
Ha! Ha! Ha! Ha! Ha! Ha! Ha! Ha! Ha! Ha! Ha! Ha! Ha! Ha! Ha! Ha! Ha!
Ha! Ha! Ha! Ha! Ha! Ha! Ha! Ha! Ha! Ha! Ha! Ha! Ha! Ha! Ha! Ha! Ha!
Ha! Ha! Ha! Ha! Ha! Ha! Ha! Ha! Ha! Ha! Ha! Ha! Ha! Ha! Ha! Ha! Ha!
Ha! Ha! Ha! Ha! Ha! Ha! Ha! Ha! Ha! Ha! Ha! Ha! Ha! Ha! Ha! Ha! Ha!
Ha! Ha! Ha! Ha! Ha! Ha! Ha! Ha! Ha! Ha! Ha! Ha! Ha! Ha! Ha! Ha! Ha!
Ha! Ha! Ha! Ha! Ha! Ha! Ha! Ha! Ha! Ha! Ha! Ha! Ha! Ha! Ha! Ha! Ha!
Ha! Ha! Ha! Ha! Ha! Ha! Ha! Ha! Ha! Ha! Ha! Ha! Ha! Ha! Ha! Ha! Ha!
Ha! Ha! Ha! Ha! Ha! Ha! Ha! Ha! Ha! Ha! Ha! Ha! Ha! Ha! Ha! Ha! Ha!
Ha! Ha! Ha! Ha! Ha! Ha! Ha! Ha! Ha! Ha! Ha! Ha! Ha! Ha! Ha! Ha! Ha!

—LORRIE MOORE, "Real Estate"

CONTENTS

This is
Salvaged

The Irates

FOR A MONTH afterward, our whole house smelled foul. There was no telling what kind of food scraps were gathering mold in the kitchen trash. What kind of unflushable sap festered in the toilet bowl. No one had the will to contend with it. One morning the smell got too disgusting to tolerate. I got in the shower and washed my hair and scrubbed my skin. I put on a T-shirt and cut-offs. I walked out of the house and up the hill and down the path to my best friend's house. I had barely left home since my brother's funeral. It was a hot, clear summer afternoon. When I knocked, Lydia opened the door within seconds, as if she'd been lying in wait behind it. My brother was dead. We looked at each other. Lydia's eyes went wet with need—she wanted to hug, I could tell. She wanted to grieve together, I could smell it on her, this desperation. She said my name—"Swati," she said.

"You look like you're crying," I said.

"That's normal, I'm sad," she said, pulling back.

"Let's go to Capitol Hill," I said. "I need egg rolls."

We walked down her street toward the main road where the bus stopped. The air was fragrant. *Blooming* seemed too formal a word for what the flowers were doing on their stems. They were doing something obscene: spurting; spilling. Sweat oozed from my skin's folds: my armpits; the backs of my knees; my crotch. I felt wet, porous, as if the world were washing in and out of me, a nudity of the soul. Lydia didn't seem to notice. At the bus stop, we stood under the shelter and waited. The bus came rolling down the street toward us, almost at our stop. I imagined stepping in front of it.

"People don't talk about labial sweat," I said.

"That's true," Lydia said. "Do you want to talk about it?" Jesus Christ—she was being so agreeable.

"No," I said. The bus wheezed to a stop in front of us. We got on and rode in silence, down the street, across the bridge, and up Capitol Hill, until we arrived at the corner where Five Happiness stood.

FIVE HAPPINESS was our favorite place—a Chinese restaurant with a yellow-and-red neon sign. We liked it because they gave out egg roll punch cards. Once you bought twenty egg rolls, you could get one for free. They weren't expensive—fifty cents each. It was possible to save up for even better rewards—fifty punches got you a carton of fried rice, and one hundred was worth kung pao chicken—but we never could bring ourselves to wait. Once, between the two of us, we filled a whole punch card in one go, and then split the prize egg roll.

It was always the same girl behind the counter selling egg rolls—girl or woman, we couldn't tell. We called her Little Happiness. She was short and plain and unsmiling, with long, oily, black hair that she wore parted in the center and pushed behind big cartilaginoid ears. Her father wore a name tag that said BIG HAPPINESS, but she didn't have one—hence the nickname. Every time we showed up, she acted as if she didn't remember us. Maybe she didn't. This time, when we walked in, I felt conspicuous, having been gone so long. But she acted the same as usual—raised her eyebrows coolly, didn't ask what we wanted.

"How many should we get?" I said to Lydia.

"Six—or eight—or what do you think?" she said.

"We'll do ten," I told Little Happiness. I took a fresh punch card from the stack on the counter and watched her punch holes in it.

We sat down at a booth, set our paper plate between us, dug in. The place was empty except for a couple of random people. One was a dilapidated-looking man we'd seen there many times before. He had a blotchy face, long white-blond hair that went down past his shoulders, and a rotating set of three or four Stone Temple Pilots concert T-shirts that he wore one after another. We had speculated about him—whether he was homeless, or worked there, or what. He mostly just seemed to sit around and eat. He could be twenty-five or forty-five—no less than twenty-five, though. He was the kind of man you felt like you should avoid.

At another table, a mother ate with one hand while cradling a child with the other arm and nursing it. You couldn't see the child's face, but you could see the mother's entire breast, including a bit of her nipple. The man in the Stone Temple Pilots T-shirt kept stealing glances at it.

My mom had recently framed a photograph of herself nursing my brother. I told her that her nipple was visible, and she said, no, it was only her areola. "That's part of the nipple," I said. I told her my brother would have agreed. But my mom thought my brother would have found it beautiful. One problem was that no one could check with Karthik. Another problem was that it depended on which version of my brother you asked. A living person is large, multitudinous. When a person is no longer living, those left behind are not up to the task of re-creating them; it can't be done. My brother hadn't been a sentimentalist. Our dad used to call him the Public Intellectual. He read a lot and liked to argue politics at the dinner table. We thought he'd be President. When the World Trade Organization met in Seattle, he organized a group of high-schoolers to skip class and march in protest of globalization.

He was so beloved and so respected that our principal not only gave her blessing but called the editor of the town newspaper, a friend of hers, and suggested that she write it up. This was when my brother was in remission. Everyone was so joyful then, so proud, as if the remission had been another one of his victories—he had been a swimmer, a soccer player, president of the Key Club, valedictorian-to-be. Even while in treatment, he'd gotten straight As. His teachers would come to the hospital with a pile of papers; they'd stay in the room while he took the exams, they'd look away only when he paused to vomit. Now he was a local hero.

He tried to explain globalization to me, he tried to get me to care. Throughout history—he said—the powerful had conspired to become even more powerful, and now it was growing more out of control than ever. He pointed at my jeans, from the Gap, my thick oversized sweater, from Abercrombie & Fitch—"all of this," he said, indicating my outfit, but then sweeping his hands out as if referring to everything, all material existence, "is part of that." It relied on people without power being forced to work nonstop under dangerous, inhumane circumstances; it relied on building factories in their villages that pollute their air, their water. How

4

this all mattered to him was a mystery to me—how it all mattered to him given what he'd gone through. The newspaper printed a photo of the protest on the front page: my brother's head bald; his mouth shaped in an O; the top two buttons of his flannel open so you could see his collarbone jutting. A new millennium was coming. He would make it through.

Later, though, it returned—his cancer. It crept into the new millennium along with us. Toward the end, Karthik sat on the couch and held forth for everyone who came over to see him. The meaning of life was to find your own meaning. Viktor Frankl. He could no longer swim laps, kick a ball around. The cancer and all the rounds of treatment had shrunk him; he had never been in remission long enough to get his muscle back. Even his nose had been reshaped into a delicate nub. He looked like a stranger. This stranger sat on the couch like a little mouse, and everyone gathered around, rapt. Now he was treated as something even more than a hero—as a prophet. He was studying religion: the Bhagavad Gita; the ancient Buddhist sutras; the Old and New Testaments. Everyone had to find their own meaning, within their own constraints. His meaning was to love us and be loved by us. This satisfied him. He was at peace.

It was that version of my brother who might have found our mom's nipple beautiful.

I wanted to tell Lydia about my mom's nipple—I wanted to see what I'd need to do to get her to stop being so agreeable, so careful. But when I turned to her, I could see she was distracted. She was pretending to focus on her food but was watching the man in the Stone Temple Pilots T-shirt as he watched the nursing woman. You couldn't see his eyes clearly because he was wearing sunglasses. He looked like an uglier version of Kurt Cobain. Lydia seemed frightened.

"What?" I said.

"Let's go, man," she said.

"I'm still eating," I said.

"I feel weird," she said.

I gestured at the man. "What, because of him?" I said. I said it loudly, on purpose. He looked over and smiled. He took out a tube of ChapStick, which he smeared on his cracked lips. He held it out to me and then Lydia, with an awful smile, and when neither of us took it, he retracted it and put it in his pocket. "I think we're too old to be pedophiled," I said, smiling in his direction. We were not beautiful—she with her acne; me with my eczema— but neither was he.

The man took off his sunglasses and hung them on his T-shirt. There was nothing special about his eyes. They were brownish. "How old?" he said.

"Eighteen," I said. We had never spoken to him before.

Lydia took some hand sanitizer out of her backpack. We had discovered hand sanitizer at the hospital, when my brother was in treatment. They said we should all use it to avoid making him sick while his immune system was suppressed. Now Lydia couldn't get out of the habit. She squeezed it onto one of her own hands, then onto mine. She seemed to have become brittle in our time apart, as if her grief had sucked all the juice out of her. We had been best friends through my brother's illness. She had slept over at the hospital with me, many nights. My brother had protected her, when we arrived in high school for freshman year, just as he'd protected me. He had found us at lunch, sometimes, and peeled us off from our table to take us to the snack counter and buy us hot, soft Otis Spunkmeyer cookies. He had handed us both our first beers and taught us how to drink them, to be chill, not too much at once. When his audiences gathered—the teachers who would come to visit, the friends of our parents, the old babysitters who had found out about his illness and turned up to say their goodbyes—we would sit and listen. But he also helped us with our geometry homework, our physics, our French. We were only fourteen.

"Rub," Lydia said.

The man stood. "It's a mistake to use that," he said, coming toward our table. He had a scratchy voice, as if he had something stuck in his throat. When he came over, he took the hand sanitizer from Lydia's hands. He had dirt under his fingernails. He sat in the booth next to Lydia, across from me. He was so close he could lean forward, flick out his tongue, and lick my nose. "It'll only make you and everyone else in the world sicker," he said. His breath smelled like milk. "That's a fact. That's God's truth. You can look it up on the internet."

"The internet," I said. "That bastion of accurate information."

"Well, it's a fact," he repeated.

Lydia shifted on her seat, and her thighs made a smacking sound.

"That's not my fact, baby girl," he said, turning to her. "That's the universe talking. That's God's fact." He looked from her to me and back to her again, as if he were trying to figure us out. "You need work?" he said.

His name was Orlando Rossi, and he had been searching for a couple of girls like us. He had been searching all over the place, and now here we were, right in front of him. Fate, he said. He was a businessman. The headquarters of Happiness Services, the business he ran, sat right above this restaurant. He said the fat man who owned the place—Big Happiness—was his girlfriend's dad. We understood who his girlfriend must be. I looked over at the counter, where the girl who sold egg rolls stood. She was taking a batch of napkins out of their plastic wrapper, paying us no attention.

"Did you just graduate, then?" Orlando said. He had returned his attention to me.

"Yeah."

"No luck finding work yet?"

"We're looking," I said.

Lydia made a face at me. Orlando turned to her. "You're not looking?" he said.

She gave a tiny shrug, didn't return his eye contact. "We're looking," she said.

THE ROOM upstairs from Five Happiness was small and lit with fluorescent rods. The ceiling was so low that you could stand on your tiptoes and touch it. There weren't any windows, just posters on the walls. Some had photos of eagles and rivers, with inspirational quotes beneath. On another, a girl straddled a surfboard, her breasts tumbling like grapefruits from the tiniest bathing suit. In the center of the room, one long plastic table was set up with beige computer monitors that had telephones and headsets hooked up to them. The only sound was the buzzing of the fluorescent lights. The only smell was egg-roll smell.

"Have a seat, mademoiselles," Orlando said, but there were no chairs. He leaned up against the table, and, after a while, I hoisted myself up onto it next to him. The porous feeling had returned to me, the naked feeling. Lydia stood across from us, her arms crossed.

"We call your girlfriend's dad Big Happiness," I said. "She's Little Happiness."

Orlando laughed delightedly, like a child. "That's an *amazing* nickname," he said. "Should I tell her? I'm trying to figure out whether she'd like that or hate it." He explained that he had wanted to propose to Jing for years, but her father—though he had plenty of his own demons—wouldn't let her marry someone who was slightly flawed by virtue of being unemployed. Big Happiness had made Orlando a deal. If he could start a business in the upstairs room and turn a profit, he could marry her. So he and Jing were starting a phone-services business together.

"Telemarketing," Lydia said.

"Sort of."

I started laughing. "Telemarketers are creeps!" I said.

He laughed, too, as if I hadn't just insulted his line of business—as if I had in fact complimented him. "I guess I'm a creep, then," he said.

I laughed again.

"I love your moxie," Orlando said. His dirty hand dashed out and tucked my hair behind my ear.

"Swati," Lydia said. "Stop it."

"I didn't do anything!" I said. "He did it."

Orlando watched Lydia, to see if she would scold him, too, but she didn't. "We're just having fun," he said, his voice childish again. "We're just playing."

"Orlando, how old are you?" I said.

"How old do you think I am?"

"You could be twenty-five"—he smiled as I said it—"or you could be forty-five. You have one of those faces."

"I'm twenty-five," he said.

"Tell the truth."

"Twenty-five!" he said.

"You made us tell you how old we are," I said.

"That was for legal reasons," he said. He explained. One of the businesses he and Little Happiness—Jing—planned to start was a phone-sex hotline. It wasn't because they were perverts. It was because phone sex was more lucrative than any other business. You could charge a lot for it. That's why it had been important to confirm that we were eighteen. He wouldn't start us on the phone-sex line—we had to earn that, he said. We had to start at the bottom and work our way up. Something about how he said it made me wonder again if he was a pedophile. He really could be. He had potential.

WE STARTED the next morning. Orlando set us up at side-by-side stations, with headsets connected to a computer that automatically dialed the phone numbers for us; for each call, the computer monitor showed some information, in blocky green text on a black screen, about the person we were supposed to be talking to. Age, race, profession, income, how often they answered our calls, how long they stayed on the line each time, what they'd bought in the past.

We began, that morning, with gardening magazines. We sold only a couple—five of them, between the two of us, mostly to old ladies who didn't seem to understand that they were buying anything. A lot of the people we called were old ladies, because the system focused on people who regularly picked up their phones, Orlando explained, and those people tended to be old and ladies. He had been listening to us and gave us some tips. For example, when the person picked up, he said, we should talk to them as if we already know them—"Hey, Rebecca, what's going on?" or even, "Rebecca!"—to throw them off guard and make them think it was a friend on the line. The tips worked, especially that one. At the end of the shift, Orlando said we'd done well, it was a good start. He sent us downstairs and said to tell Jing to give us each a free egg roll. Jing did.

After that, we returned each morning and stayed eight hours. We sold more magazines, along with kitchen gadgets and decorative tchotchkes. The saddest was a gig calling people up and telling them they had won a free trip to Hawaii. They would get excited about it until we explained that they hadn't quite won yet. First they had to watch a promotional film about home improvement. Then they would have a *shot* at winning: no guarantee, but it was a good shot.

Not that the gigs were all bad. Our favorite was a magazine about Native American history; selling it made us feel like we were doing a good deed. We had to phone strangers up—we called them leads—and convince them to accept a free issue. Once I called an old man with a hard, mean voice. "I don't read magazines," he said.

"But this will teach you something," I said. "It'll tell you how the Native Americans lived before white people arrived."

"I get my history from the *Bible*, sweetheart," he said, and hung up.

I told Lydia about this on the bus ride home, and she cracked up. I hadn't seen her laugh in a long time. I thought she was starting to enjoy herself. I get that from the Bible, sweetheart! we said. The Bible, sweetheart! we said. The Bible!

I wasn't religious. My only relationship with the Bible was that my brother sometimes read to us from it. He read to us from everything. The readings were soothing, like lullabies. Anyone—he said—could feel God's love. You didn't have to be a religious person; you didn't have to believe in one version of God. I didn't buy it, but Lydia did. She'd grown up Christian. She'd lapsed, somewhat, but my brother was bringing her back around. She was relieved that my brother believed, even if he wouldn't commit to one particular god—this was probably enough to get him to Heaven. We hadn't talked about it, but I knew she imagined that he was up there now, watching us. I thought that might be why she was so careful, so tentative, all the time—and so judgmental of me.

Before all that, when my brother had only just been diagnosed, Lydia and I watched a movie about witches and decided to become witches. Every year on the same night—I can't tell you which, because we promised we never would tell—we sat in candlelight with the soles of our feet touching, wrote a wish apiece on scraps of looseleaf paper, crumpled each of our papers into a ball, dripped hot wax on the balls, and hid the balls in a shoebox in my closet. We both wished for my brother to get better. When he found the box and we explained the concept—just the concept, not the actual wishes—he made fun of us. He thought our crumpled-up wishes looked testicular. We called them waxballs, but he pretended to forget their name. Your little sackballs, he said, your precious sackballs.

Then he died. Afterward, my parents undressed him and cleaned him with a washcloth. They went over his face and his stomach and his armpits and his crotch. His sackballs, his precious sackballs. He still seemed almost as if he were sleeping. My mom told me to choose an outfit to put on him. I chose my favorite flannel of his—the one he had worn to the World Trade Organization protest, the one in the picture where his mouth was a big O. By then he was starting to seem dead, his lips puckered and hard and blueish. When my mom and dad tried to put him into the flannel, his limbs were too stiff, they couldn't do it between the two of them, so I held his arm up while they got one sleeve on, and then the other arm while they did the other sleeve. We all picked him up and carried him to the living room and placed him on the couch. I sat down on the carpet next to him with my hand on his forearm.

One by one, people came over. When there was a critical mass of Indians at our place, the aunties sang loud, mournful songs. It seemed like a performance to me. It seemed like they were showing off. Our white friends couldn't tell. They were moved. I sat there in the same position, holding on to my brother's arm as it cooled. I stared at the cracked leather of the couch. I counted the lines in the leather. Only when Lydia showed up and called my name—her voice high and trembling—did I stand. I got up and ran into her arms, and we stood in the front hall shivering together like that, and I loved her. Then I sat on the other couch with her, across from the couch with my brother on it. I closed my eyes and let her braid my hair. It felt nice. But then she stopped braiding my hair and went over to where my brother lay, to where I had been sitting before. She put her fingers on his arm. She murmured something, a religious chant of some kind. I hated her, then. I can't explain it.

When my brother was alive, our parents used to make sure all my hours were accounted-for. Even when they were at the hospital, I had to call the nurses' station with my whereabouts at any given moment. If I even walked to the gas station, I had to make it known. Now that my brother was dead, no one cared where I went each morning. I wondered if they wondered.

I thought about whether Orlando Rossi might be a real pedophile. I thought about whether he might be a murderer. Lydia's aunt had once been asked on a date by the serial killer Ted Bundy. She said no, so he didn't get a chance to kill her. If Orlando tried to kill me, I knew what I would tell him. You can rape me, but please use a condom, and please don't kill me. My brother died of cancer last month, and if anything happens to me, my parents will be destroyed. Maybe he would still kill me. If there was an afterlife—as my brother claimed there was, though I didn't believe it—I would go and search for my brother there. If there was not an afterlife, that would be the end of me. It wouldn't be my fault. I would have tried not to get killed. Lydia would escape and tell my parents I had tried to stay alive.

EVER SINCE we had become Orlando's employees, though, he had been acting less like a pedophile and more like a boss. We were the first employees he had ever hired. He told us this with pride. We were paid minimum wage, plus a $1 commission for each conversion. We were never supposed to hang up before the lead hung up, with one exception—the people Orlando called the Irates. The yellers, the swearers, the demanders of managers. The Irates. I liked the sound of them. "I want an Irate!" I told him. "Give me an Irate!" He laughed. Lydia laughed.

But what I wanted most was to work the phone-sex lines. It wasn't fair, I told Orlando, that he hadn't started us on that yet. The rest of it was getting boring—the retirees, the stoners, the stay-at-home moms. When I passed his desk, I grabbed him by the hem of his S.T.P. shirt and tugged. "Come on, don't we work hard?" I said. "Aren't we model employees?" This made him laugh, but he promised nothing.

We did work hard. We were model employees. We got on the bus in the morning and didn't return till after dinner. We gave ourselves goals and surpassed them. Ten conversions in eight hours, then thirteen, then fifteen. Orlando taught us more tricks. It turned out he'd gotten into this business because he used to be a telemarketer himself, at a place down the street; that's how he had met Jing. Lydia and I pooled our commissions and, at the end of each afternoon, spent it all on fried rice or kung pao chicken. Only the egg rolls were free, and Little Happiness was becoming stingier with them. When the end of August rolled around, Orlando took us to see her. He said he had a promotion in mind for us—he said it with meaning. But he had to ask the boss. When he walked us up to the counter, Little Happiness stared him down. It was the first time I'd seen any expression in her face; it was fierce. He tipped his head toward us and said, "Come on, let's do it."

"They're not legal, dumbass," she said. I'd never heard anyone say it, *dumbass*, the way she did; she pronounced the *b*, which made it sound like a more powerful insult than usual.

"We have ID," I said, more to Little Happiness than to Orlando. "You can see it." We didn't, but I figured we could buy fakes off some corner on Broadway, or whatever people did.

Little Happiness acted as if she hadn't heard me—as if I didn't exist. "If you got us in legal trouble, my dad would murder you," she said to Orlando.

Orlando sighed performatively. "Would you stop being a bitch?" he said. "It's a highly profitable business."

She snorted—bitchily, I thought. "Fine, let one of them try it, and keep the other one on Hawaii, the tchotchkes, whatever," she said. She looked us over. She was tougher than I'd given her credit for being. She was in charge here, she'd been in charge all along. "Give it to whichever one of them has the better voice for it."

"What kind of voice is better for phone sex?" he said.

"Sweet," she said. "Like—soft, sweet. You'll figure it out, babe."

"Jing," Orlando said. "Do you have anything to eat?" He said it gently, as if he were the one auditioning to work the phone-sex line.

She gave him an egg roll. Then she gave me and Lydia one each. We followed Orlando back upstairs. The dynamic had shifted. Orlando seemed smaller. I wondered if Lydia noticed. When we got upstairs, Orlando said he needed to hear our voices. He needed to try us out. We should do it one at a time, he said. He looked at both of us, as if trying to decide who should go first. Then he told Lydia to wait downstairs awhile with Jing.

"You've got to be kidding me," Lydia said, but she followed his instructions.

Orlando closed the door behind her, then sat on the table and gestured for me to stand in front of him. I remembered the time he tucked my hair behind my ear. I'd been trying to get him to touch me ever since, but he hadn't. I stepped close to him. "No, don't," he said, taking me by the shoulders and pushing me away. "This is about your voice, baby-girl."

"What about it?"

"You need to show me that you can appeal to anyone. Our customers are from all across the nation—all walks of life. Name a profession that lets you meet such a diverse group of people."

"Is this the tryout?"

"Yes, ma'am."

"President."

"Name a profession that people like us could actually get," he said. He said it as if we were people like him. As if we were—the three of us—in the same situation. As if we had spoken to him in the first place for some reason other than that my brother had died and my house smelled rancid.

"We could be Presidents," I said. "Lydia and I."

Orlando widened his eyes and laughed. "'Lydia and I,'" he said, imitating me. "See, you come across as stuck-up right there—most people would say 'Lydia and me,' but you said 'Lydia and I.' That's why I'm marrying Jing. She's got street smarts, she's tough, she doesn't care about status, she wouldn't want to be a President. She's gone through hardship."

"I've gone through hardship."

"Ha," he said. "What hardship?"

"My brother died!" I said.

He made an unreadable face. "Is that true?" he said.

I didn't know whether to answer—I felt like I'd said too much.

"Maybe your brother died," he said, as if he were deciding whether to believe it. "But Jing—that's a whole other universe. Jing is an only child. Her dad loves her, but he's too hard on her; she only has him, her mother died when she was really young."

Mothers die, I thought. Everyone's mother dies at some point.

"That's bad by itself, but that's not it—have you heard of the Guangxi Massacre? You haven't, I don't need to wait for your answer—they don't teach anything in public school, I went through the same system. It was part of the Cultural Revolution, which I hope you've heard of—you'll have to know about that if you want to be President," he said. "It was terrible. There was cannibalism involved in some places, they found out later; they killed people and ate them. Jing's mom was killed as part of that. Here's the stupid part: She didn't do anything; she was a housewife, she didn't care about politics. It was him—Jing's dad, the asshole—who got drunk and made some comments at a restaurant when the waiter was listening. Jing was there when they took her mother—they came looking for her father, and he was out drinking again, so they took her mother instead. Jing's grandmother was there, too, and her mother supposedly told her—Jing's grandmother—that when her father came home, he should take Jing and immediately escape. I don't know if that's true. If it were me, if I were taken by the police because of something my husband said, I'd want him to come get me out of there and turn himself in. But he took Jing and ran off to Hong Kong, and no one heard from her mother again, and after a while they had to assume she had been killed. Jing was a baby, she doesn't consciously remember any of it. A couple of years later, they came here, to Seattle. But these memories stick with you in your bones—that's God's truth. She doesn't let it get to her. Her dad bosses her around, but he's still an alcoholic. She's the brains behind all of this."

"Her mother was *cannibalized*?"

"No—but people were, other people. With Jing's mom, no one ever heard anything more about her."

Then Jing's mother might still be alive, I thought. She might have escaped from prison and disguised herself so she wouldn't get caught. It's possible she tracked them down a long time ago and has been staying nearby all this time, following them from Hong Kong to Seattle, watching Jing grow up. It's possible she's secretly their next-door neighbor and is just waiting for the right moment to reveal herself. And even if not—at least Jing didn't have to watch her die.

"I'm trying to get to know you better," he said. "If your brother really died, this is one of those moments in life when it's important to be open, honest. Like—what happened? What were the circumstances of his death? Do you understand why it's important to be open like that?"

I looked at him. He was flushed; he seemed out of his depth. "It makes a person good at phone sex," I said.

Orlando blanched. "No!" he said. "Come on, man!" He shook his head. He looked at me for a while, as if waiting for me to say more. I didn't. Finally he sighed and went to the door and opened it and bellowed Lydia's name.

"Hey," I said. "What did you mean about those moments in life? What moments?"

"It's Lydia's turn," he said.

"What do you want to know about it?" I said. I felt a bit desperate. "Tell me—I'll answer whatever you want."

When Lydia came up, she looked at me questioningly, but I didn't respond. Orlando told me to go downstairs, but I didn't want to hang out with Jing. I was afraid of her—she had my number, she could see through me. I also wanted to try to hear Lydia's audition. I wanted to hear what she would tell Orlando Rossi about my brother. Orlando shut the door, and I sat on the landing at the top of the stairs and smelled the egg-roll smell and tried to listen. I could make out Lydia's voice but not the words. She didn't sound any different from usual. She just sounded like herself, talking.

LYDIA GOT the promotion. After that, we still sat next to each other, but while I talked to stay-at-home mothers and retirees and unemployed people, Lydia talked to perverts. I could see why Orlando had chosen her, not me. She sounded young, helpless: "I've never done that—can you tell me how to do it?" And I, next to her, like an idiot: "But don't you want to learn how the early Americans lived?" Or: "It's a shot at winning, a *good* shot!" I felt my hatred of her growing. Soon, I thought, it would be larger than my love for her.

September came around. We were supposed to start school again soon. Then one morning, Lydia called to tell me that planes had flown into the Twin Towers in New York. I didn't know what to make of it; I'd never been to New York, I didn't know anyone who lived there. When we arrived at work, Orlando hugged us. "You're okay?" he said to us. "You're okay?" I told him we were fine, but Lydia glared at me. We weren't fine, she said—she and her mother had been crying all morning. At my house, no one had cried. We had been surprised, but none of us had cried. "Oh, baby doll," Orlando said to Lydia. "I hate hearing that, though." He was starting to like her more than me, I could tell. I had asked him, over and over, what made him choose Lydia and not me for the promotion—what made her sexier than me. He said it wasn't about that. He said that, to be good at phone sex, you had to project sensitivity to the other person's needs. Lydia, he said, could do that.

Orlando had the TV on, without sound—we could see the people on-screen screaming and bawling, but we couldn't hear them. These people weren't even relatives of the people who had died. They were regular people, witnesses, who had been walking down the street when the buildings collapsed. Dust had landed on some of them. Maybe some debris. Now they screamed and bawled as if they had some claim to the dead.

I turned on my monitor, put on my headset, looked at the screen. I was supposed to call someone named Ernest Jackson— an eighty-three-year-old African American man, according to the screen, living in Atlanta. He had recently agreed to watch the promotional video about home improvement in exchange for a shot at a pair of plane tickets to Hawaii, but he hadn't shown up at the screening center.

The person who picked up, on the first ring, had a tense, barking voice—I couldn't tell if it was a man or a woman.

"Oh, hey, Ernest!" I said, guessing.

"Not Ernest," the person said.

"Oh, you sounded like Ernest there for a minute," I said.

"I sounded like *Ernie*?" It was a woman.

"Well, could you put him on?"

"Baby, what's this about?"

"The plane—"

"Oh no—is this about our daughter?"

"Well, no, I'm looking for Ernie—is he there?"

"She's in New York—she lives there, she's a nurse for old people. I tell her, come on home, you can be a nurse for this old person, me. But she likes it there."

"It's possible her phone isn't working," I said. "But if you could tell Ernest—this is about Hawaii, it's not about New York, it's about the flights to Hawaii, he talked to my colleague about them."

"Hawaii!" she said. "Ernie did serve there—you're with Veterans' Affairs, then?"

"No, I'm not, ma'am, I'm with Cascade Services, Ernest won a chance to get a pair of tickets to Hawaii, he just had to visit us and watch a video, and he didn't show up."

There was a pause. "Cascade Services," she said. "Tell me again, what is this? You're saying Ernie won something?"

"A pair of flights to Hawaii—I mean, it's a chance at winning, but a good chance. We're inviting him to watch a short film, and after that, he'll be entered in a drawing. Half of everyone wins."

"Where are you calling from—are you in America?"

"Seattle."

"And you've seen the news, there in Seattle." Her voice had gone cold.

"The TV is on here, at work—it's on silent, but I'm watching."

"You're watching—and *all the same*, you people decided to give me a call about a flight on this particular morning, when I'm waiting for the phone to ring and for it to be the only child I'll ever have in this God-given life, telling me she's all right?"

"Well, no, I'm calling Ernie," I said; I'd gone cold, too.

"Baby, don't play with me," she said, in a warning tone.

"Put him on, please. I need to talk to him."

She made a sound then. I couldn't tell if she was laughing or what. "You know what?" she said. "*Me, too.* I've been needing to talk to Ernie for the past three months." She was crying a little by this point. "Understand? He's not going to be needing your *plane tickets.*"

I understood. She could have come out and said that her husband was deceased, and I would have marked it down and hung up. It happened all the time. I began to laugh.

"What's that?" she said—but she half growled it, an animal sound.

She's getting mad, I thought. Irate, I thought. Hang up, I thought. But I couldn't. I had that feeling again, the feeling of having no boundaries, of the world swishing in and out of me. I had started to sweat, hard. "Old people die," I said. "He was eighty-three, old people die, it's normal." I couldn't hear anything on the other end—she'd gone quiet, though she was still on the line. Suddenly my sweat grew cold on my skin. I could sense my own borders again. I felt afraid of Mrs. Ernest Jackson. I hung up.

Lydia shot me a terrible look. I paused the monitor, pulled off my headset, set it on the table in front of me. I was freezing; my legs felt weird. "I got an Irate," I said. Lydia didn't hear me, or pretended not to. "I'm sweating, but I'm cold," I said. "My legs are tingling." Lydia pressed her palms to her ears, as if trying to block me out. "Anything—just tell me," she promised, softly, into her headset. "Yes, sir, anything," she said. The smell of egg rolls suddenly disgusted me. I had traveled a vast distance to escape my foul house, only to discover I hadn't escaped the foulness at all, it had followed me here. It would follow me—I was beginning to understand—everywhere I went.

ON THE bus ride home, we were both in awful moods. I leaned my forehead on the seat in front of us. The leather was cracked;

it smelled salty. I didn't want to look at Lydia. She kicked the seat in front of us. It made my forehead bounce. "Quit it," I said, and I sat up and shoulder-checked her, but not hard.

She stamped a foot. People turned to stare. She said my name—"Swati," she said, spitting it. "You think you're special, but you're not. There's a whole world outside of your existence. Karthik is the one who told us that."

I sat still, staring forward, and felt my heart pounding at its cage. Poor Lydia. My best friend. I could punch her heart out. I could bite off her limbs and masticate them and swallow them. I could annihilate her. I would do it. If that would return my brother to this earth—give me an airplane, and watch me ride it through her. Through Jing, through Mrs. Ernest Jackson. Each building on this planet. Each mountain. The last God-given atom on earth. I would destroy it all.

I took a breath and let it out. I turned toward her. "Maybe he told you that you're not special, but he never told me that," I said. I said it bitchily—I said it like Jing might.

Lydia's face crumpled into an expression I had never seen on her—pain mixed with disgust. "You *smell*," she said.

"It's not me," I said. I was surprised; I thought I was the only one who smelled it. "I've been smelling it, too, but it's not me."

"It is," she said. She grabbed me by the shoulders, turned me toward the window, unzipped my backpack, and rooted around in it. That's when she found it. An old egg roll, at the bottom of my bag—I didn't know how old, whether it was from the summer or even earlier. It had turned brown and misshapen inside its plastic wrap. Sackballs, precious sackballs. Lydia took it and pulled her arm back. She was going to smack me in the face with it—I could feel it. I was electric with anticipation. I closed my eyes and waited for it. It was what I wanted. But instead she dropped it on the floor of the bus and kicked it under the seat in front of us. "See—it was," she said. "It's okay, though," she added. It sounded like her mouth was wet, gummy—a mouth full of grief.

That night I wrapped myself in my sheets and closed my eyes and pretended I didn't exist. But in the morning, the sunlight came through my shroud and forced me awake once again. I was a living person in the world of the living. All I had left was you people. The doorbell was ringing. It was Lydia, calling through the door that we were leaving for the bus stop. We had better get moving, or we would be late.

I, Buffalo

THE EVENT IN question took place at the end of the summer. I don't recall which day. That summer the days failed
to distinguish themselves from one another, and given that failure, I don't see why I should do the distinguishing for them. I
can tell you that this anonymous day opened warmly. I know
this because I began the day on the bus and recall perching
on the edge of the seat so that my thighs wouldn't stick to the
plastic. I had woken early and, unable to sleep, decided to go to
the park.

The only other people on the bus were a young woman and
her son, who sat in the row of seats across from me. The mother
wore a fur coat and a firm expression, and the boy perched on her
lap facing me with the hem of his mother's coat tight in his fist.
He might have been four years old.

"Hot day for a coat like that," I said to the mother.

"Pardon?" the mother said defensively, as if I had cast an
accusation.

"Hot day," I said. "I'm going to Golden Gate Park."

The mother ignored me. The boy fidgeted and squirmed on her lap and, finally, his mother said tiredly, "Baby, you want a grenade?"

The boy turned toward her with delight and nodded.

"What do you say?" she said.

"Mama. Give me a grenade."

"Nuh-uh. What do you say?"

"Please, Mama. Give me a grenade."

The mother seemed satisfied with this. She said, "All right," and reached into her purse.

As I watched her fumble, I realized I was sweating. The heat was part of it, but I was also starting to feel anxious. I had my hand on the bell cord, ready to pull at any time, as if it were some sort of alarm, but when the mother drew her hand from the purse and opened it to the boy, her palm was empty.

"Here you go, baby," said the mother.

The boy took the imaginary grenade, pulled on an imaginary pin, and the next thing I knew, he had his eyes fixed on me and his arm pulled back. A gasp flew from my lips, and one of my own arms threw itself up in defense. I put it this way because they, the gasp and my arm, seemed to act of their own accord. I never would have reacted like that on purpose. The boy froze, then turned to look at his mother, who rubbed his shoulder and shook her head at me.

"Child's just playing. Good God."

"I'm sorry. I've got a hangover."

I've always had a habit of sharing too much with strangers and demanding too much of them in return. In my youth, my mother coached me against this, and for a long time I held back. But over the past eight months, my opportunities for conversation had been limited.

"I don't drink," the mother said through pious pursed lips. "Haven't in five years." She indicated, with her chin, the boy.

"That's good," I said. "Nothing good comes of it." I added, "You hear stories like that—a woman has a child, and it saves her life." I wanted badly for the mother to think well of me. "I like your coat," I said, when she didn't respond. I also wanted badly to know about her choice to wear it on so hot a morning.

But she didn't respond to that, either—only pushed a big horse's breath of air through her nostrils, then moved her gaze toward the front of the bus and sat silently.

Nothing good does come of it. I wasn't lying about that, nor am I lying about anything else that happened that day. I haven't lied since I took an oath, long ago, to behave in a manner consistent with the truth. At the time I found the language strange— that I behave not necessarily in a truthful manner but only in a manner consistent with the truth—but after a while I got used to it. That was a long time ago. Still, I know some facts consistent with the truth.

I am a woman.

I am thirty-four years old.

At the time of the event, my apartment had recently been vacated by the others who had formerly inhabited it with me—a forty-four-year-old man from Oregon and a sixteen-year-old dog of unknown breed. The man was a hopeful and bighearted man who demanded much goodness of others and was therefore often disappointed. I trusted him completely. He had taken the dog, too. They left behind them a great and holy void. It resembled the alarming emptiness that cathedrals and mosques hold for those of us who believe in nothing beyond what is proven to exist. We feel ourselves surrounded only by unfilled space. That's where I lived at the time of the event.

I awoke on the afternoon of the event to the smell of spoiled fish and a fierce headache. I could remember nothing of what had transpired between the bus and my awakening. Not a single detail. The morning on the bus seemed as far away as another continent. This was not, I'll admit, an altogether alien feeling. I'll be direct. I've blacked out many times in my life. I was a teenager when it started. I'm ashamed of this. Any addict who says she's not ashamed is lying to you or to herself. It makes matters worse if you don't fit the stereotype. You spend your days all tucked into your white shirt and pressed pants and iron-flattened hair like a perfect productive citizen. It's not a lie—it's not as if colleagues say, "Are you an addict?" and you say, "No way!" Still. *Fraudulent*—that's probably the term.

But now the smell of spoiled fish brought a couple of details back to me. At some point earlier in the day, I recalled, I had opened a take-out box of sushi and a bottle of wine. I had finished both. I had vomited. That's all I had.

My apartment has two floors, which makes it sound larger than it is. I woke in my bed in the bedroom, which is upstairs; the door was open to the hallway, and it seemed that the smell was coming from out there. I ventured into the hallway and found that my hunch was correct: here, the smell was truly noxious, as if the entire marine world had died and washed up into my apartment. I felt a prick of recollection: Something had gone wrong. I hadn't reached the toilet in time; I hadn't reached a garbage can; I hadn't found my way to the kitchen sink.

But where had I done it, then?

Downstairs, the smell was fainter. In the kitchen, the sun shone warmly onto the countertop. The sky that afternoon was fogless and clear and blue. I checked the living room, ducking to inspect the fireplace for good measure, but saw nothing. I felt better—clearheaded and alert—as I went through these motions, but as soon as I recognized this, my anxiety welled up again. I'd been through enough afternoons like this. I knew the hangover had only gone dormant. It would surely come alive at some point in the evening. Good God, I thought. How had I slept so long?

That's when my sister called. They were on their way up from Los Angeles for the weekend.

"Who is?" I accused.

She and Sam and Mara, she said. Who else? Right now they were outside of Tracy.

"You're staying here?"

"If we can?"

"Did they put you up to it?"

"Oh my God. Are you serious? Hold on. She's being paranoid—she thinks our parents sent me. Hold on. Mara's got an audition. She's excited. Sam says we'll be there in a couple hours."

"Fine."

A little voice sang out in the background; my heart leapt to catch it.

"Mara wants to know why you don't want us to come."

"Tell Mara it's because I know you have ulterior motives."

"She doesn't know what that means, ulterior motives. Hold on. Nothing, Mara. She says she does want us to come, she can't wait to see you. Hold on. Mara wants to know what's for dinner."

"Dinner?" I said. "Pizza?"

"Takeout?"

"No. I don't know why you'd assume that."

"I'm not assuming anything," Priya said. "We get takeout all the time."

"It's not takeout," I said.

Because I know how to make pizza. In fact, I'd already had the idea earlier that week at the grocery store when I came across the pre-made dough sitting next to the hummus like a bagged breast. I picked it up and decided to choose good tomatoes and make the pizza sauce myself. To make good pizza sauce, you have to pick tomatoes that smell a certain way, according to an Italian friend of mine—yeasty, my friend said, almost like beer. So I held a tomato to my face and sniffed. The tomato smelled only like itself, tomatoey. I grabbed another one and smelled, then another, then another. My mind latched on to this one word, *yeasty*, and wouldn't allow me to move on. Yeasty, said my mind, yeasty, and finally I just settled on the best-looking tomatoes, the reddest and closest to bursting, and continued to the meat department. All of the ingredients had been sitting in the fridge ever since, as if they knew this day would arrive, when I would be called upon to make dinner for my sister.

By the time I hung up with her, I'll admit, I'd forgotten all about the smell. I started making the pizza. I chopped the tomatoes. I rolled out the dough. I had a great satisfying sense of being a civilized person in a civilized world. Only when it was all ready to go did I pour myself a drink. A glass of wine. I can handle, you understand, a glass of wine.

Then evening arrived. At the sound of the doorbell, panic rose in my throat. I lit a vanilla-scented candle and set it on the kitchen table. The candle had already burned down nearly to the bottom. When I opened the door, and Mara came bounding inside and took a running leap into my arms, I can't explain the feeling I had. I want to call it euphoric. But I know how that makes me sound. As if this might have been the onset of some kind of episode.

"Sheila Auntie!" she said into my shoulder.

"Mars Bar!" I said. I'll tell you—I had nearly forgotten how much I love this child. My Mars Bar. When was the last time we'd seen each other? I never saw her anymore. I put her down—she'd gotten heavier since I last saw her—and took a good look at her. She was wearing what looked like pajamas—a dinosaur-patterned jumper with built-in footies. Sam and Priya stood shoulder to shoulder in the doorway. They were the same height and had grown to look alike over the ten years of their marriage—the same mildly skeptical smile, the same slight stoop of their shoulders. "Let's play!" I said.

"It's almost bedtime," Priya said.

"She has to wake up early for the audition," Sam added.

Mara is a child actress. She auditions for all sorts of roles. I knew they sometimes traveled. But San Francisco? What kind of a film got made in San Francisco? Who had ever heard of that? Once Woody Allen made a movie in the Haight. A colleague of mine saw him at Zam Zam. So maybe this wasn't only a pretense for checking in on me. Maybe our parents hadn't put Priya up to this after all. I started to relax. Then Sam sniffed at the air, and I felt a sharp synaptic twitch as I remembered the vomit.

"Come in, come in," I said to them all. "Give me your sweater," I said to Priya. "I like your sweater."

Et cetera.

I was trying to distract them from the smell.

"Give me your sweater, give me your bags," I said. "Give me all of it—I'll put it up in the room. How was the drive?"

They didn't give me any of it. "Don't be so formal," Sam said. "We'll take it up, no problem."

But the smell, I told myself. But you don't want to act weird, I answered myself. "Whatever you want," I said.

While they went upstairs with their bags, Mara wandered around the living room, picking up various objects—a snow globe on the bookshelf, a framed photo of me and my ex that I couldn't bring myself to take down—and setting them down again. She wore enormously thick eyeglasses, and her hair was done up in a pair of uneven pigtails. Glasses aside, she looked strikingly similar to how Priya had looked as a child, despite Mara's bland ghost of a father. I suddenly remembered another part of what had happened between morning and evening.

"Hey, kiddo," I said, "you want to see a buffalo?"

"I've seen buffaloes," she said.

"Are you sure?" I said. "Real buffaloes?"

"They have them at the zoo," she said.

"This is different," I said. "These ones are in the park."

Because that's what I had done that morning. I was on this kick. I had been treating myself to the sights of San Francisco that I had been too busy to visit during my working life. When I got off the bus, I stopped and bought a little bottle of bourbon. The smallest, cutest bottle. A child could hold it in one fist. The bourbon glowed from within like liquid sun. It took all my willpower to put it back in its paper bag and hold that bag tight till I got to where I was going. Good God, it was hot. When I arrived at the paddock, I was drenched in sweat. There were supposed to be nine of them—three adults, six calves, all female—but I saw only one. She had the top-heavy build of a boxer—this barreled chest, these meaty shoulders, this impenetrable wall of a forehead, all balanced on top of four matchstick legs. For her to stand on those legs and get from one place to another should have been impossible. It defied all good sense. Yet that's what she did. She walked with true grace, as if nothing mattered but to walk. Her shoulders pumped with strength. Her legs tottered only a little. When she came to a patch of yellow grass where some wildflowers had sprouted, she stopped and lowered her head as if for benediction. She was massive and shaggy and humpbacked and ancient. Her grace made me feel like the smallest of creatures. She ate the flowers.

I pressed my face to the grid of the wire fence, cool against my skin, and I called out to her. "Hey, girl," I said. "Hey." She ignored me. Truly, it was as if I weren't there. And maybe I wasn't, I started to feel. There was not another human being in sight. Only me and the great animal. Who was I to allege that I existed? For what reason should I exist? Where was the proof?

And it's true that it was hot out. And it's true that I was sipping from my bottle. But the strangest thing happened. Having eaten, the buffalo raised her head again, and I felt a great topspin of joy at this. She continued her walk, in my direction. She was so close I could see her eyebrows, and this, too, seemed miraculous. An instant later, she tumbled to the ground on her side as if felled. Her body sent up a puff of brown dirt. And in that moment, I felt as if I had fallen to the ground myself. I could taste the dust in the air. Every filament in my body relaxed. I was not a thinking being. I was free.

Mara came across as very comfortable in her skin, the way child actors often do. "You want to know something interesting?" she said.

"What?"

"The Donners ate each other. You know them? The Donner Party?"

I was taken aback. I hadn't remembered her being this gruesome. By the time I thought of what to say—"Not personally," I wanted to say, to be a little funny—Mara had moved on. She was wandering around the room, occasionally asking a question: "Who's this?" Or, pointing the remote control at the TV, "How does this work?" She moved really fast. I couldn't keep up. "Sheila?" she said after some time.

"Yeah?"

"What's that smell?" she said.

I froze and then recovered. "What smell?" I said. "Must be your upper lip."

OVER DINNER, they explained that Mara's audition was for a film about the Oregon Trail. Mara had been doing her research to get into character, getting Priya to take her to the local library and search the catalog. That was how she had discovered the story of the Donners, who had eaten each other.

"I wouldn't eat you," I said to Mara, "unless I was really hungry."

"Dude!" Priya said.

I chewed on a pizza crust, took a swig of beer, and grabbed another slice. I had fled Mara's question about the smell by giving my flippant answer, then running to the kitchen to put the pizzas in the oven. Now all seemed nice again. We'll go see the buffaloes tomorrow, I thought. Maybe tomorrow the others will be out. I would say to Mara, "Did you know that the American bison is the largest mammal in North America? Technically, they're bison. At one point there were sixty million of them in the United States alone. That was before the United States existed. Then white people showed up and hunted them so bad that there were only a couple hundred of them left. They were about to go completely extinct. So some environmentalists got together and decided to save them. They put a bunch of them in Golden Gate Park, and maybe some other places, too, and all these bison had babies, and now they're not even close to going extinct." All of this was true. I had been surprised by this information, which I'd found on a big, faded tablet in the park.

"Do you know what *extinct* means?" Priya asked Mara.

"It's when every single animal of one kind of animal dies," Mara said.

"Right," Priya said.

"Like the Donner Party," Mara said, and grinned.

"Oh God," Priya moaned. "Sam."

"I mean, not exactly, Mara," Sam said. "Humans won't be extinct until we're all dead." He turned to me. "She does this great cannibalism routine." He took a giant bite of his pizza and chewed with his mouth slightly open. A little cheese sprayed from between his teeth. "Nom-nom-nom," he said, and when he finished, he patted his stomach. I laughed. He had grown one of those soft, domestic paunches. My own, lost man had one of those. A place to cup your hand at night. A place consistent with the truth if ever there was such a place. My God, I had gotten so close. "Method acting," he said—this other man, Priya's man, said it.

"Don't make fun of me!" Mara shouted, dropping her pizza onto her plate. It seemed she might cry, but then she started laughing shyly.

"Don't mess around, you guys," Priya said. "Sheila, Sheila, this gruesomeness of hers, it's actually freaking me out. How long until it isn't a phase anymore?"

At first I felt a surge of pride that my sister would still confide in me, after all that had happened between us. The truth was this: I had been a bad big sister, full of spite. I would persuade poor Priya to watch as I stretched a live worm with my fingers until the creature snapped in two or allowed a mosquito to rest on my thigh and fill itself up with my blood before thwacking my palm onto it and smearing the resulting reddish gunk across Priya's shirt. But our parents had ignored this, in light of my excellence at school and in piano lessons, and had focused on berating Priya for her learning difficulties and clumsy musical efforts.

But then I recognized what was happening. She must have been waiting to find me in a moment of weakness. Here was that moment, and here was her chess move: How long until it isn't a phase anymore? The implication being that there was a direct line between my own childhood badness and my recent fall from grace.

Oh, that.

Fine.

I might as well tell you about it: the so-called fall from so-called grace. My scandal involved a high-profile, married client. He had been in San Francisco on business for a day and a night, and we had agreed to meet for a drink at the martini bar atop his hotel. We were supposed to discuss a case involving asbestos in a housing complex in the Western Addition, but after a few drinks, we discovered that we had both spent part of our twenties in Shanghai, and suddenly we were trading obscenities in Mandarin. I turned to look out at the sunset. This was a historic hotel, the kind of place at which girls were said to have sat in their sailors' laps before sending them off into the cold Pacific mist, and, thinking of this, I slid my hand across the table until my fingertips rested atop his own.

I don't know what to say.

I was in a sort of fix with respect to my man.

We had been together for three years. But recently he had proposed to me, and after this, I had found myself hating him. I hated him for wanting to commit himself to me forever. He was the only person who knew me to my core. Yet he would have himself committed to me forever. Was he some kind of idiot?

I had accepted, of course.

But now this.

Before long, my client and I were back in his hotel room, and

I was sharing with him several lines of cocaine. Then we were jumping on the bed. We were touching the ceiling with our fingertips. We were having so much fun. I was biting his thigh. This was a foreplay move that my man with the dog liked. My client was making these sounds. My client sounded different from my man. He also looked different. He had a massive orb-like stomach and a pink coloring. He brought to mind Santa Claus.

I was considering this idea and enjoying the fun of it, my teeth against Santa's skin, when I realized that my client was sobbing. It embarrassed me; I had mistaken his boyish little gasps for noises of anticipatory pleasure.

"Could you just hold me?" he whispered.

The fun seemed over far too quickly.

But I shimmied up the bed's twisted sheets and allowed him to lay his bearded head on my chest and whisper about how little he loved his wife, whom he respected for her intellect but with whom he had no romantic chemistry. His tears and snot salted the valley between my breasts. But the kids were still young. They were all he had. He pulled his phone from his pocket. Would I like to see some pictures? On Facebook? Maddie at the beach. Rico on his birthday. It was for them that he made his living taking advantage of the vulnerability of undocumented immigrants, because, we might as well both face the facts, lawyer and client, this was what we were doing. "I plead guilty!" he said. "Ha-ha!"

At this, my horror was complete. I finally stood and retrieved a hand towel from the bathroom and dabbed forcefully at his tears and snot.

"This didn't happen," I said. "I swear."

My indiscretion was discovered within days: due to a slip of the finger, the client accidentally sent a drably suggestive email meant for me (he couldn't stop thinking about my mouth) to the office manager at my firm, who was also named Sheila. Soon after that, the client confessed all—I have no idea why he did such a thing, but he did. I was fired. Of course, I had to tell my man. You know the rest, about his departure with the dog, and the emptiness.

It was the cocaine that turned them all against me. I guess it was his first time. People could say about the other behavior: Well, it happens to the best of us. But the best of us don't introduce drugs to our law clients. The best of us—maybe you're among them—feel that if attorneys, who take an oath to behave in a manner consistent with the truth, go around introducing their clients to drugs, then everything is permissible. Well, what if it is? Can there be a fall, I ask you, if there is no grace?

I went to the sink to refill the pitcher of water and contemplate how to respond to Priya's comment. "That's how kids are," I said, when I returned to the table. And I feinted: "In fact, just this morning on the bus, a little kid tried to throw a fake grenade at me." After freezing like a little statue, his arm pulled back, the boy had dropped his hand to his thigh. While his mother had spoken, he'd filled his cheeks with air and slowly expelled it, meanwhile drumming his fingers on his leg.

"It's crazy," Priya said, "how many irresponsible adults there are in this world."

None of us spoke. We bent our heads over our pizzas, we munched our crusts from end to end, we pinched between our fingers the bits of sausage and pepper that had fallen to our plates and ate those, too. Sam sighed and went to the fridge for a second beer.

Priya burped. "Oh God," she said. "I'm tipsy."

"Are you kidding?" I said. "You're not drunk."

I hated those women who would have two drinks and claim to be wasted. Oh, my delicate constitution! I couldn't believe my little sister had turned into one of them. She used to be fun; she used to be able to keep up with me. Our parents worried more about her than about me. No matter how much she studied, she couldn't do better than a B average. No matter how much she practiced piano, she couldn't progress. And now you looked her up online, and she had this slick social media presence. She had once been an up-and-coming journalist, but she left that when Mara was born; now she made YouTube videos about being a stage mom, or whatever you call it. She got invited to write guest posts on parenting blogs. Meanwhile, an online search for my name turned up lurid articles in the legal press. I held out hope that other, more prominent people with my name would soon overtake me on Google. Most of them were unlikely candidates: a self-published poet in Virginia, a teacher in Detroit. But some seemed promising. I had my eye on the marketing vice president at Proctor & Gamble who, according to LinkedIn, had been slowly moving up the managerial chain. I prayed for the rise of that other, better Sheila.

Now Mara spoke again. "Sheila, seriously—what's that smell?"

Priya and Sam turned to look at me, and I stood to clear the table, making a noisy pile of the plates and then going to the sink to slide the scraps into the garbage disposal. I could feel pinpricks under my arms, and I wondered if I was visibly sweating. "What?" I called out from the sink, but even as I spoke, I knew I sounded stupid. I had to confess. "The smell?" I called, still standing there. Then I returned to the dining table and added, like it was nothing, "I threw up somewhere."

"Oh, Sheil," Priya said. I didn't know which was worse—her passive aggression minutes ago, or her pity now.

"I don't know where it is," I said, feeling smaller than the smallest person ever to have existed. "It's weird."

There was silence. Then Sam said, "That's okay!" He grinned. "That's okay, Sheil! It happens to everyone."

Priya opened her mouth as if to protest—it does not happen to everyone—but Sam had already scraped back his chair and rolled up his sleeves. "We'll help you," he said.

I wandered around the kitchen. Priya was drawn to the laundry room.

Mara went upstairs by herself. Soon, she cried out, "Found it!" We went scrambling up the stairs to where she stood peering down into the laundry chute. That dark limbo space of the house.

"Mara, move it!" Priya cried out. This was dirty business. Grown-ups only. Mara stepped back at the sharpness of her mother's tone, and the rest of us crowded around the laundry chute to see. Mara was right. The vomit had dried mid-drip along one side of the chute into a purplish brown crust of yellowtail, tuna, and fish eggs, decorated with rice globules and seaweed bits.

"Whoa," Sam said.

And suddenly—just like that—I remembered.

I had found myself, after visiting the buffalo, in the BART station downtown. How had I gotten there? I don't remember. It was rush hour. I felt strange to be there among these working people—these weary, bowed-backed working people, their fingers working their phones as if they were rosary beads: they who I once had been. They were not identical. I don't mean to suggest that they were. They were in fact quite the opposite—each of them so very different from one another, their private concerns theirs alone. One woman sat on a bench with an accounting textbook open in her palm. She pressed the other hand to her forehead and mouthed the words as she read. People passed by and didn't notice her, nor did she notice them. They were like trees to one another, or pylons in an obstacle course. I felt ghost-like that morning, as if I had escaped the world of the living and was now paying an invisible visit. I felt as if I had acquired important knowledge that they all lacked. And by the time I arrived at my stop, I was happy. Yes. Happy. I picked up some sushi and wine. When I returned home, I set the radio to play through all the speakers in my house, and I went up to my bedroom and ate and drank. There was a French song on the radio. It was a nice song. The lyrics went something like, "Eska poo poo yay yay yay! Voo sashay la moonay pay!" I stripped and dropped my clothes to the floor, and I went through the closet, putting on outfit after outfit. I stood before the mirrored closet door and shimmied and sang. "Eska poo poo yay yay yay! Voo sashay la moonay pay!" I stood in my pile of clothes, and I trembled and sweated and felt joyful. I lifted my breasts and felt the cool air on their undersides. And then I felt nauseated.

"Of course Mara was the one to find it," Sam said. "Your sense of smell hits its peak when you turn eight and declines when you hit your twenties." How Sam loved to make perfect sense out of everything strange and mysterious in the world. He looked at Mara, who, after her mother's rebuke, stood quietly to the side. He touched her shoulder and said, "The first step is to clean what we can reach from up here." He held the laundry chute open and peered inside. "Sheila," he said, "do you have a sponge?"

I went down to the kitchen and got the dish sponge from next to the sink, then returned and handed it to Sam.

"Sam, let her do it herself," Priya said. "For fuck's sake. Mara, stay back."

"Oh, let me try," Sam said, and he gave Priya a look that was compassionate and trite. Your big sister is in trouble; we must put aside our disgust and try to help. Scrubbing with the dish sponge, he loosened and cleaned the crust around the top edges of the chute, and the fish smell tangled with the lavender scent of the detergent. But the vomit had dripped deep into the chute. Sam couldn't reach far enough to get all of it.

"I'll try," Priya said, avoiding my eyes. She took the sponge from Sam and stuck her arm into the chute, twisting at the waist to reach as far as she could. Her shirt lifted as she stretched, and I could see the light down of hair at the small of her back. Sam touched it. How bourgeois, I thought, for a husband to be tender toward his wife. "I can't get it," Priya said.

"My turn," I said. But I couldn't reach, either.

The problem was that the space was too small for us; we were stymied at the shoulder. Priya had the idea to go downstairs to the laundry room and try to reach the vomit from below, and she took Sam with her to investigate while I stayed upstairs. Soon I heard her voice bellowing up through the chute: all they could see were some drops of puke atop my towels in the laundry basket. "It's too far," Priya called. "It's all up there."

From the top of the chute I could see her poking a broomstick around. It made a hollow rattle. Mara crept closer, her eyes aglint. Was she thinking what I was thinking? I bent to her and waited for her to say it.

"I could try," she whispered.

"You want to?" I whispered.

"I can?" she whispered. She touched her mouth.

"Shush, they'll hear. Let's get you in there." I handed the dish sponge to her. What I did was, I hoisted her up by the waist and let her shimmy into the chute. I held her by the thighs, then by the ankles. "Go at it, sweet pea," I said. Only then—when I had her by the ankles, all of her weight in my hands—did I remember how heavy she had become. A full-grown child. I felt it in my forearms. I felt it in my back.

"Gross," Mara said in a voice that seemed echoey and overlarge.

"Mara?" Priya sang out from the laundry room—two trembling notes, rising low to high. She could probably see Mara from down there. I don't know why she said it as if it were a question. Mara didn't respond. She only grunted like a mechanic.

"Sheil?" Priya shrilled. Her voice rose. "Mara? Sheila?"

Then came Priya surging up the stairs with Sam on her heels. "For God's sake, pull her up, Sheila!" she cried. I hoisted Mara out by her ankles and deposited her on the carpet. Priya swooped in and picked Mara up in her arms.

"Mom, I'm fine," Mara said, and squirmed out of Priya's grip. "Gosh," she said. She smoothed her hair and scanned the faces of the adults. The scent of lavender swelled in the hallway, and for a moment it was all I could smell.

"Done," Mara said. She sniffed and smiled. "Actually, I love vomit," she said.

"Good girl," I told her.

But I suddenly felt worn out and dirty. I felt vomit on my palms; I felt it in the air.

Back downstairs, we washed our hands in turn. We didn't speak. We didn't make eye contact. We sat on the couch. The Donners ate each other, I thought.

"Priya, I want to make you a martini," I said.

"I'm wasted," she snapped.

"You're sleeping here!" I said. "Who cares?"

"I'll have one," Sam said.

"Sam," Priya said.

I felt impatient. I went to the kitchen. I made three martinis and brought them back on a tray. Sam took one. Priya hesitated. Then she took one, and I did, too. I felt great as soon as the gin touched my lip. It was like swimming in a long, deep pool and finally getting to the end of the lane. You come up for air and feel great before you've even taken a breath, because you're anticipating all the breathing you're about to do. That's how I felt.

Priya was just holding her drink in front of her. "Sam, actually, take mine," she said softly. "I don't want it."

"Oh, babe, I don't think I can," he protested. "Don't drink it, then."

She glared at him. I knew what she was doing. What she was doing was straight out of some textbook. Some idiot's guide. She knew I would finish her drink if she didn't, and she wanted Sam to have it instead so I couldn't. But I felt great and would not be made to feel less great. "I'll have it," I said, and I took the glass right out of her hand, and I had it. Right there, on the spot, I had it, and when I returned to my own, I felt triumphant.

I sat back into the couch, drinking mine, and watched Mara. She was building a fort. She had pulled a cushion from the armchair and taken it to the wide space near the fireplace, where she dropped it. Now she went to the dining room table and got a heavy, tall-backed chair, which she carried, struggling, to the living room. She returned and got another, then another. All these she arranged into a tight enclosure. Finally she came and squeezed onto the couch between me and Priya and regarded her creation.

"Nice fort, kiddo," I said, reaching down to swipe at Mara's ear.

"Hey. It's a cave."

This struck me as a great thing for a child to say, smart and original. Not a fort—a cave. I wondered what other thoughts were whirling around in my niece's head. I thought about all that I erroneously believed in my childhood: if you don't brush your teeth at night, they will rot and fall out; blowing your nose in a towel will leave a dark stain that can never be removed. But Mara could not be deceived! "It's a cave," Mara had said. "I love vomit," she'd said. I was struck hard by the force of my love for this child. Every other love of my life seemed small compared to this love. I put my drink down—emptied—and grabbed Mara by her arm, pulling her to me. "You're perfect," I said.

"My arm," Mara said. "Stop."

"Sam," Priya said. She seemed tired and sad.

I let go. "Don't ever grow up," I said.

"Okay," Mara said. She rubbed her arm, then scampered across the room and ducked into the cave.

"Remember how we used to do that?" I asked Priya. "We used to make a fort and pretend to be wild animals living in there?"

"I wanted to be the lioness," Priya told Sam. She was doing that thing where she was pretending I wasn't part of the conversation.

"No. You liked being the boar. I did your hair."

"This one time," Priya told Sam, "she did my hair in a braid and then she took the gum out of her mouth and wrapped it around the bottom of the braid instead of using a hair tie, and our mom had to cut it out."

"Oh, come on," I said. "It wasn't tragic," I told Sam.

"It was horrible," Priya said. "It was deranged."

Mara crawled out from her cave. She surveyed the room, plucked a knitted blanket off the armchair, and put it over the front opening of the cave. Then she disappeared again.

"She has an artist's mind," I said. "I was thinking tomorrow we could take her to Golden Gate Park."

"Can't," Priya said to Sam. "The audition."

"After the audition?" I asked.

"Maybe?" Sam said to Priya.

Priya squirmed. "There's something under here." We all stood, and Priya lifted the couch cushion. There, among the lint and the hair, was a brown apple core. Frankly, I couldn't remember the last time I had eaten an apple. Yet there it was. Proof.

"Oh God, Sheila," Priya cried out. She tucked a loose strand of hair behind her ear and wrapped her arms around herself as if she were cold. Then she put her hand to her mouth. I realized she was crying. She was really crying. She was going at it. It occurred to me that I had rarely seen her cry, even when we were kids. She had always, underperformance and all, been composed. So this was alarming. A grown woman. The sight of it exhausted me. I leaned back into the couch cushions and closed my eyes. "I'm going to sleep," I said. "Good night."

There was silence for a while—then Sam consoling Priya. "Shh," he whispered. "She's okay."

I actually thought for a moment they were talking about me. I felt touched. I felt, for a moment, that all was not lost. I almost opened my eyes. But they weren't talking about me. "She could have broken her neck," Priya said. "Jesus Christ."

"Let's get some fresh air," Sam said.

I could sense Priya hesitating. Then, in a small voice, she said, "Okay."

I swear to you, the sound of my baby sister's voice. It reached inside of me and ruptured time. I wanted to say something to her. But I didn't know what any words could accomplish. "I love you." How stupid. How insufficient. I couldn't. I don't even know what she looked like in that moment. Still, I felt so close to her. I don't know if she felt it. I guess she didn't. She went over to the cave and peeked inside: "She's sleeping, too," she said to Sam. Then they went to the door. They put on their shoes. They opened the door. They went out. They shut it. All was quiet.

I opened my eyes. I stood. I sat. I stood again, stumbled, and fell to the floor. Water, I thought, and I went crawling to the kitchen. This was a good way to get from one place to another. I'd forgotten how good. I hadn't crawled in a long time. When I got to the sink I stood, steadied myself, and poured myself a glass of water. I drank. The water tasted healthful and mineral, as if I were sipping from the palm of the universe itself. The palm of truth. Your palm. I drank. I poured another glass. I drank and drank. I felt desperate. I remembered that I had shed my clothes earlier in the day and stood in the pile of shed clothes and sung. Now I mourned that moment and all the others that had died. I placed my glass on the counter and knelt on the floor, and once I was there, it seemed impossible that I could stand again. So I didn't. I got on my hands and knees. I padded across the kitchen and into the living room. My shoulders pumped. I felt nothing but the instinct that I was to go to the cave. And when I arrived there and pulled back the blanket and peered inside, I found what I had known, on some level, I would find. There emanated from inside the cave—in the person of the child inside, may you bless her and keep her ever safe—the hot radiance of truth.

The cave was warm and dark and smelled of honey. The child lay curled on her side, her arms tucked at her chest, her cheek pressed to the floor. Her mouth hung open as she breathed, and a thin thread of drool dangled from the corner. Her bowed mouth was of the reddest red. I moved carefully into the cave, not touching the walls, and remained on my hands and knees before the sleeping child.

But I shouldn't say *I*.

I wasn't there.

The buffalo gazed upon the child and felt at peace. The child's eyelids fluttered, and her mouth made little movements, and the buffalo held her breath and stayed still. Then the buffalo let herself fall at the child's side and rolled so their bodies were close.

She wanted to be closer still. She pressed her chest to the wings of the child's back, and she cupped in her paw the round of the child's belly, and she pushed her forehead to the child's soft neck, and she wept. For she had been alone for so long. And now this child, with her warmth and her goodness and her sweet smell. Oh God. Did she hold the child too close? Did she make some sounds that a child might find frightening? From outside the cave came the distant sound of a door opening and closing. The sound of a person calling the child's name.

What can I tell you?

An instant later, all would be lost—the walls of the cave torn asunder so that all the goodness and warmth dissipated; the child's mother flying in, reaching to pull the child out from the buffalo's grasp. What more is there to tell? Good God, I would tell you if I were the buffalo, let it be. Enough with all these words. Enough with the endless questions and endless answers. It's cold down here in the kingdom of man. Let this one child's heat warm a creature against the dying of her species.

This Is Salvaged

MARLON HAD REACHED the point in life—the midpoint—at which time starts to run out. He had grown up poor and forgone art school, less because he couldn't afford it, though he couldn't, than because he didn't know such an option existed. It was true that he'd come up in life. He wasn't unsuccessful. He had won awards over the years, had been exhibited, had been invited to give lectures to pale, serious, twig-armed students on midwestern college campuses. The problem was that he made installations, which were difficult to sell in general, and on top of that, his particular installations were meant to be impermanent: He built them out of feathers, sand, leaves, human hair and waste—his medium being the fragile and perishable—and, rather than binding them together or preserving them with the usual substances, glue or shellac, he arranged a room with his materials, in as correct a formation as he could figure out, then let them be. He envisioned the art degrading as people interacted with it, until it transmogrified into something else altogether. Often, though, a piece would stay intact for weeks because no one had wit enough to touch it. To explain that they were supposed to touch it, to instructionalize the message, would defeat the purpose.

During the summer of the midpoint—the midpoint's midpoint—it all came to a head. He filled a large white-walled room in an art gallery in Aspen with a giant sand castle that rose nearly to the ceiling, impressed with intricately arranged strands of his wife's black hair that he'd dustpanned up from the bathroom floor. People were meant to kick the castle. Tug at the hairs. But no one did, until finally a couple wandered in with their toddler, and the child nudged a small bridge, low to the ground, with his little sneaker. It collapsed. The parents cried out in mortification, then blamed each other, then went to find the gallerist, who explained, laughing in relief, that this was the point of it all. The point being that in the future none of this would exist in any recognizable form, its component parts scattered into some yet-unknowable configuration. Marlon didn't mean just the art. He was referring to the extinction of all terrestrial life. The universe continuing on even after we had all been atomized and wind-scattered.

It wasn't supposed to be serious. It was supposed to be comical—an anxious and rageful type of comical, but comical nonetheless. People were meant to laugh! Instead, after the couple learned the point and returned to the exhibit space to spread the word to other gallery-goers, they all made grave little muttering sounds, then set about pinching and prodding at the structures. The piety of it all. The problem was that art patrons were rich, which twisted up their sensibilities. They had lost so little, so seldom, that they were inexperienced at handling it; they stood stiff-backed and solemn before loss, believing—maybe from the movies—that this must be the right pose. Normal people, the poor and poorish masses who had lost much and lost it often, knew the truth, which was that you had to laugh. But normal people, by and large, didn't care for art galleries. He realized all this now, but he hadn't always known it. He hadn't spent enough time with rich people, before he started showing his art, to know how different they were from normal people, and by the time he began, it was too late.

He and his wife had been living in Fort Collins, where she worked at a hospital and he taught occasionally at the state university. Irina had married him because she had found him charming at first, and he had married her because he loved people precisely to the extent to which they found him charming. The trouble was that charm, by its nature, wears off; successful charm involves an element of surprise, which time erodes. They used to have a game in which Marlon would ask, "Are you mad at me?" and Irina would run over and cover him with kisses: she wasn't mad at him, she would never be mad at him! But after a while, she changed the rules. He would ask, "Are you mad at me?" and she would clench her face at him and respond in Russian, her native language, a phrase that had no direct English translation but meant something like, "That's enough, let's change the subject," and he would have a grim feeling that she was gathering the courage to leave him, like all those women before her.

These days, Irina worried about money. She kept pointing out that they were closer to the end of their working lives than the beginning. She had tried to convince him to look for more consistent employment, in product design, for example, and when he refused, she had suggested that they move to Modesto, California, where several of her Russian nurse friends lived well. She brought it up often, and each time she mentioned the town, it sounded to him like she was screaming it. Modesto! Modesto! Even its name proclaimed its meagerness. Sometimes he felt murderous. To avoid murdering her, he decided, a couple of days after the incident with the toddler and the bridge, to leave. He took his savings out of the bank, in cash, put half of it in his wallet—thirty hundreds—and packed his truck full of sketches, note-books, clothes, his bike. Irina was sleeping because she worked odd hours at the hospital. She would come home at noon after a twelve-hour shift and wouldn't wake till dinnertime. So he did all this unnoticed. He wrote a note and put it next to her phone: "I couldn't take it anymore, which isn't to say I've killed myself," he wrote. "For a wild surprise, look outside!" Then he laid half of his cash—the other thirty hundreds—on the front lawn. He got into his truck. As he drove, he imagined her out on the lawn in her cerulean nightgown, her hair wild, clutching armfuls of bills against her chest and realizing she missed him.

That night, as he slept in his truck in the parking lot for a trail that ran alongside the Poudre River, he dreamt that the Poudre had flooded, but instead of sinking, his car had risen up with it and floated. He had climbed out the window and onto the roof and paddled with his hands, rescuing stranded citizens as he went. When he woke up, his nerves felt sharp-edged, somewhere between anxious and exhilarated. It had started raining in the night. It was still raining. He got out of the car and, in the rain, posted a video about his plan to build an ark.

It would be a real ark based on the specifications of the King James Bible. The project would take three years to complete. He would employ unhoused people for the construction, and, upon completion, it would be moored and would host rotating exhibits on climate change—all this to meet the requirements of his big-gest funders, a real estate developer that had pledged to eradicate homelessness and an oil corporation committed to a lower-carbon future, who had stepped up, along with the other funders, after his video was shared by an evangelical Christian influencer and went viral.

Marlon arrived in Seattle—he had chosen it for its large unhoused population and its proximity to the water—on a mid-summer morning, clear and warm. He parked on the street in front of the Christian shelter with which he'd negotiated an unusual arrangement: he'd live there for the duration of the project while also employing the shelter's residents. The evangelical church that managed the shelter was another one of his funders. Two older men sat on the crumbling curb. Marlon wondered how he must seem to them, stubble-faced and flop-haired and smelling sour—like one of them. The men toed the root-broken road, with two cups of orange juice between them, watching him. One was heavyset and bearded, with a cheerfully authoritative air; the other was thin and scowling and bald. The heavyset one pointed to the bed of Marlon's truck and said loudly, "Good-looking bike."

"Hey, thanks, bud," Marlon said.

"You hardly ever see a bike with fenders like that."

"Don't I know it," Marlon said.

"You're the artist?" the man asked.

"Indeed," Marlon said. He was surprised the man had identified him as such.

"Glenda said you'd be coming this morning," the man explained. "We're supposed to greet you. I'm your foreman—Manny. And this," he said, gesturing at the other man, "is my best friend. Buck, introduce yourself."

Buck muttered, looking at his feet, "You already introduced me."

A small young woman slipped out of the shelter, her hands on her hips. She was the sort of woman you can't help but think of as a girl. She wore a linen dress with thin straps and had white-blond hair pulled back in a ponytail. "Is he the artist?" she asked Manny and Buck. Her voice was soft, tentative.

Marlon stepped past them and thrust his hand at her. "I'm the artist," he said.

"Marlon," she said. "I'm Glenda."

"Glenda!" he said. They had been in touch over email—she seemed to manage the place—and he had expected someone different: older, fatter, stronger. He was pleased that she was like this instead.

"I've never heard of anything like this," she said. "Is this really the kind of thing they do?"

"Who?"

"Artists," she said.

ON THE first morning at the building site—a decommissioned shipyard in the industrial district south of the shelter, to which the men could commute by foot—Marlon overturned a crate and stepped up onto it. He had a speech prepared for the gathered men, many dozens of them. It was partly about climate change and partly about Leonardo da Vinci. Da Vinci, the great artist-inventor, had come up with all kinds of machines: a proto-airplane; an armored car; a portable bridge. Toward the end of his life, he became obsessed with the idea of a grand deluge and wrote in detail about how one might be represented in art.

"Into the depth of some valley may have fallen the fragments of a mountain, forming a shore to the swollen waters of its river, which, having already burst its banks, will rush on in monstrous waves; and the greatest will strike upon and destroy the walls of the cities and farmhouses in the valley," he wrote. "Trees and plants must be bent to the ground, almost as if they would follow the course of the gale, with their branches twisted out of their natural growth and their leaves tossed and turned about. Of the men who are there some must have fallen to the ground and be entangled in their garments, and hardly to be recognized for the dust, while those who remain standing may be behind some tree, with their arms around it that the wind may not tear them away; others with their hand over their eyes for the dust, bending to the ground with their clothes and hair streaming in the wind."

Marlon read all this to the assembled men with his head bent over the paper. It was when he looked up—to explain that it was puzzling to him that, for all the inventions da Vinci designed, he had never proposed an ark, like in the Bible—that he realized he had lost his audience. The long quotation had bored them. Or maybe it wasn't da Vinci's fault; maybe his presence, da Vinci or not, was boring. He felt awkward and fraudulent.

He recalibrated, simplifying. He told them who he was and what he was there for, and he listed the specifications. "The King James Bible calls for gopher wood and pitch," he said. Historians disagreed about what gopher wood was, but a common guess was cedar, so that's what they would use. He gestured at a great pile of cedar planks against the back wall of the warehouse. "The pitch is from a Swedish supplier," he said, indicating a dozen steel vats in the corner of the warehouse. The ark would be built plank-first, the cedar set down board by board and hand-joined with pins of iron.

They had three years to build the ark—there was enough funding to last only that long. "And that's that," he finished, putting his hands in the air, looking out at the audience. Manny, recognizing the cue, began to clap. The others followed.

Marlon stepped down from the crate and asked Manny and Buck to walk with him to pick up sandwiches for everyone. He had come to understand, from Glenda, that Manny and Buck had been best friends nearly their entire adult lives. They had been staying at the shelter, off and on, all that time. Now they were pushing seventy, and everyone knew who they were—Manny and Buck, never just Manny or just Buck. Marlon envied their companionship. He and Irina had fallen out of love a long time ago, but she had been his best friend—his only friend—and he missed her. Of course, that wasn't the only reason he had sought them out for the walk to the sandwich shop. "Glenda's nice," he remarked as they left the shipyard. "She been working here long?"

Buck flashed him a silent glance, a tense, man-to-man expression that he recognized well and that ignited his competitive spirit, before Manny answered him straightforwardly. Glenda and her parents used to visit the shelter every Sunday, to ladle chili into their bowls. They belonged to the church that managed the place. She had been a tiny, timid girl—the only child who, when she became a teenager, continued to show up. Then, when Glenda was in her junior year of high school, both her parents had died within the span of a year: cancer, suicide. She'd gone to college locally and never stopped coming to the shelter, and when she graduated, she started working there. That was two years earlier. Nowadays, she knew how to sass the men when she needed to. But most of the time she still behaved like a child. She didn't speak much, and she wore the same delicate silver cross around her neck that she had always owned. Marlon wondered aloud if she'd been emotionally stunted by her parents' death. Maybe that was why she worked at the shelter, even though she could have gotten work anywhere, with her college degree. Maybe she couldn't stand to leave the life her parents had known.

"She lives there, too," Manny said.

"In the shelter—with us?"

"Women's floor."

Buck didn't engage, just glared at the air in front of him. They got to the sandwich shop. They ordered ham-and-cheeses and PB&Js and waited.

Then Buck spoke up. One afternoon, he said, not long after Glenda's parents died, he had accidentally walked in on her while she was in the bathroom. Her jeans and panties were around her ankles, and she was sobbing with her face in her hands. When she saw Buck, she asked him to come in. She told him she needed a hug, and he hugged her while she was right there on the toilet. Her body heaved in his arms, and he could smell her pee. Afterward, she pulled her pants up and washed her face. They never spoke of it again, he said, but they'd had a special relationship ever since.

"Oh come on, Buck," Manny said. "That's not a relationship." It was clear Buck had told this story many times before. Manny turned to Marlon. "It's not a relationship," he said, in a tone that seemed meant to reassure him.

Buck grew quiet again. Their orders were ready. They walked toward the shipyard in silence, each man carrying in both hands plastic bags full of sandwiches and thinking his own hard thoughts.

Construction began.

They started with the keel. Manny was in charge, with Buck as his second-in-command. The third- and fourth-in-command were Davis and Joe, who were both younger but had experience with ships, having served in the Navy. On four wooden crates arranged in a circle, they sat with their cigarettes and issued orders to the rest of the men. Marlon sometimes wandered around, sometimes sat with them. He didn't know where he fit. He wasn't a shipbuilding expert. For that, they had brought in a consultant from Texas—a Christian engineering professor whose dissertation had been about how to build a seaworthy ark, which many considered impossible. The consultant had drawn up the designs, and whenever they were stumped, they called him on FaceTime and showed him the problem. Glenda took up lunch duty, arriving each day with bagfuls of sandwiches.

One afternoon, when all five of the men were sitting together, Glenda came over wearing a sundress with a hem that hovered mid-thigh and smiled at Buck. He called her to them, retrieving a sixth crate and popping it down next to himself. "Glenda, I need to know," Buck said. "Have you ever thought about modeling?"

"Oh *gosh*," Glenda said as she sat, her eyes almost crossing. "No, Buck, never."

"You should think about modeling," Buck said. "You have straight teeth. Straight and white."

"Don't be a pervert," Manny said to Buck. "You've known her since she was six."

Buck blinked, hard, and cried out, "I didn't mean anything by it!"

"Easy, Buck," Glenda said. "I know you didn't." She patted him on the arm and stood. "It was nice of you to say it," she said. "No one ever noticed my *teeth* before."

"See?" Buck said, lifting his chin at Manny.

Marlon couldn't believe this was real. He found himself observing it all as if from some distance—from his own disheveled childhood—and admiring the aesthetics of the whole scene. The big men, the little waif. He was seized by an urge to grab her by the cross on her chain and pull her to him. He imagined the small cross crumpling in his fist. When Glenda stood, as if to leave them, Marlon touched her arm—taking care to be gentle—and said, "Hey, sit down, sit down." When she did, with a certain mindless obedience, he felt a rush of pleasure. "You're wearing a dress," he commented. "You don't see that in a shipyard too often." It was the first time he had been so forward with her.

"So?" Glenda said. "Can't I wear a dress without everybody commenting on my appearance?"

Marlon grinned and said, "Glenda, how old are you?"

"Twenty-three," Glenda said.

"Twenty-three is a good age," he said. "Do you know the writer Thomas Wolfe?"

"I don't," Glenda said.

"When Thomas Wolfe was twenty-three, he said, 'I don't know yet what I am capable of doing, but by God, I have genius—I know it too well to blush behind it.' I like that. I see you, twenty-three years old, and I think of that."

Glenda colored and coughed. "Okay," she said, as if Marlon had insulted her. "I don't know what you're getting at."

"Hmph," said Buck, casting a skeptical look of kinship at Glenda. "Genius."

"I think you do know what I'm getting at, Glenda," Marlon said, pointing at her. He laughed. "I think you do!"

THAT NIGHT, Marlon offered to help Glenda with the dinner dishes. He thought it would help her to picture him in her life, her washing, him drying. "Glenda, about how tall is this building?" he said. It was quiet in the little kitchen, the other men having gone to their rooms.

"Well, there's sixteen stories," she said. "Feet-wise, I'm not sure what that comes out to."

"Have you been to the rooftop?"

"A couple times," she said. "There's not much up there."

"I wonder if you can see the shipyard from there," he said. "I wonder if I could take some pictures. It'd be good to have some pictures for when we're done and people are wondering how it all came together."

"Well, I doubt it, but go on up," she said. "Go on up and see for yourself."

"How, though?"

"Elevator."

He went up, alone. It was a cool night. The rooftop was scattered with leaves and beer cans, as if no one had bothered to clean it in a while. In a corner, someone had left a six-pack of Bud Light. He picked it up. The cans were full, though warmish. He could see a bit of the shipyard in the distance, all the ark's scattered parts looking like wood chips. He wanted to feel something—some excitement about it—but he didn't; he was preoccupied with the fact that Glenda hadn't offered to go up on the roof with him. Maybe she hadn't understood. He picked up the six-pack. When he got back on the elevator, he stopped on the fifth floor—hers—and opened the door to the hall. Men weren't allowed. He moved down the hall softly calling her name. A door opened. Glenda stood there in an old-fashioned nightgown, similar to the sort Irina wore. It had frills at the shoulders and ended at her ankles. Her hair was wet.

"Marlon, what is it?" she whispered.

"I found this on the roof," he said, holding up the beer.

"Beer," she said.

"It's not allowed, right?"

"I can take it." She held out a hand. "You've got to get to your room."

"What's the rule?" he said.

"You can't be on this floor at all," she said. "You shouldn't be here."

"I mean the rule about beer."

"Marlon, come in real quick. I'll get in trouble."

He entered the room and shut the door behind him. Though the room was similar to his in style—scuffed green carpeting, popcorn ceiling, dim light—it was much larger, with a couch instead of a bed. They must have special rooms, better than usual, for the staff. It smelled of coconut, and he told her that.

"That's my shampoo," she said, and she lifted her wet hair and looked at it.

"Maybe," he said. He stepped toward her. She didn't move. He bent his head over her hair, which she still held, and put his face in it and breathed. It smelled excellent.

She stepped back.

"Glenda," he said. "Come on, let's have a beer. I won't tell."

"Well, it's allowed for staff," she said. "I've had beer."

"Technically, I'm staff, too," he said.

"No, you're not. You're the artist-in-residence." She smiled.

"That's what they call me," he said, though he had come up with the title himself.

"Whisper, then," she said. "We can have a beer, but don't be so loud."

"Do you have ice?" he whispered.

GLENDA HAD never had this kind of attention from a man—a man from the outside world. Maybe I've changed, she thought. Maybe I'm finally growing up, I'm not stunted anymore. When they sat on her couch with their beers, she curled her legs and arranged herself so that her toes touched the depression in the back of one of Marlon's knees. Marlon pointed out that Glenda didn't have a bed, and she explained that the couch pulled out. She had given the bed to a resident and replaced it with this couch so that, during the day, she could have more space.

"I've never had this kind of attention from a man," she said.

"That's a lie," Marlon said. "I've seen you get attention."

Her face burned. "When have you seen that?"

"Buck, for one," he said.

"Oh, Buck," she said, rolling her eyes, and they laughed.

They discussed whether Buck had a crush on Glenda—Marlon said he did, Glenda disagreed. Glenda felt tipsy, and she told Marlon so. He said he did, too. She couldn't tell whether he was telling the truth, whether it was normal to feel drunk after one beer or whether it took more than that. She told him this—she told him she doubted him. She felt like she could tell him whatever came to her mind and he would be interested in it. She told him she didn't drink much, because of her faith. She told him that all that she did in life resulted from her faith. When she had received the email from her pastor—the email about the ark—it had been faith that had compelled her to accept the artist-in-residence request. She admired the influencer who had shared Marlon's video. When Marlon showed up at the door, minutes ago, with that six-pack of warm beer and she let him in: that, too, was faith. He seemed to her like a man unmoored from meaning—a lost man—and she felt she had been called to care for him. She thought about telling him this, too, but stopped herself. She sensed she would have to be less forthcoming about that part.

"It's an amazing feeling, to feel like your choices are being driven by a power greater than you," Marlon said.

For a moment it seemed as if he had read her mind. "You're not religious, right?" she said. She was hopeful, though.

"Oh God, no," he said. "But it was almost a religious feeling, for me, when the idea for the ark came to me. And now it feels like it's happening with almost no effort at all, like it was meant to be."

"Ha!" she said, trying to hide her disappointment. "Let's see if Manny and Buck and all the other guys agree. Let's see if they feel like it's no effort at all."

Marlon laughed. He punched her lightly on the knee, then kept his knuckles resting there. They grew silent. His fingers stretched and spidered. He inserted the pads of his fingers into the sweaty crook of her knee. "Anyway," he said softly. "I can help you pull out the couch if you want."

They stood side by side, and together unfolded the couch into a bed. It was the first time anyone had ever helped her with it, and she thought, joyfully, This is why people get married. The shelter's shared bathroom was a few doors down, and they each took turns wearing Glenda's pink flip-flops and padding down the shelter hallway to pee. When they were both back in the room, Marlon pulled off her nightgown and underwear and folded them with reverence, placing them neatly at the foot of the mattress. Then he pulled off his own shirt and pants and underwear. They sat kissing and putting their hands in each other's hair. They grew bolder. They lay down and clutched each other's shoulders and thighs. Glenda was a virgin but had seen enough sex in movies to have a rough sense of it. She was worried about the way her breasts would flop to the side if she lay on her back, and would hang, pendulous, if she climbed on top of him. But she did hunger for him. He was such a large person, she such a small one. How delicious it would be to consume him into her body. How satisfying. But then, it would be painful, too. She went back and forth, desire to fear to desire to fear.

Marlon turned Glenda onto her back and moved himself over her.

"I'm a virgin," she said.

Marlon paused, midair. He had not entered her yet. Seconds passed. He removed himself from above her. "Is there anything you want me to say about that?" he said.

"No, but thank you for asking," she said.

"Should we stop?" he said.

"Oh no, that's all right."

"I think I'm in love with you, Glenda," he said, and returned to her. "I've known a lot of girls, and I've never felt like this in my life."

By THE end of a year, they had the frame—a great jutting rib cage, like that of some long-forgotten sea creature, four hundred and fifty feet long, seventy-five feet wide, and forty-five feet high. The men began laying cedar planking around the hull and pushing pitch-coated oakum into the seams. Manny stood down below and boomed up at them with his megaphone. "Keep it even. Get in there, Ted, to the left, to the left, there." From down below, the men looked small. A faint tarry smell hung in the air. Glenda was Marlon's girlfriend now. Most nights, he snuck into her room and slept there with her.

On the night that the upper decking was completed, they walked down to the shipyard with blankets and climbed inside. It was dark in there, the smell of the pitch sharp in Marlon's nostrils.

"Look at all this," Glenda said, grinning. "This is God's work."

She had been bringing up God more often as their relationship progressed. She had told him she wanted to marry a Christian.

"You have to put everything you've got into it," Marlon said. "Whatever it is—put everything in. That's the only way to be an artist."

"I'm not an artist, I don't care about being an artist, that doesn't matter to me, I'm interested in listening to God's will." Glenda smiled at him. It seemed to him that a small gap was opening between them. He recognized the feeling. He'd had it before, with other women—where it became clear over time that your agendas had diverged, or that maybe they'd been different all along, but one or both of you had hidden it well for a while. Still, she was smiling. So he smiled, too. She laughed, and he laughed. He backed Glenda up against the bulkhead, and she wrapped her arms around his waist and then, remarkably, her legs around his own. He thought he might stumble and fall, but he steadied himself and kissed her. "This is it, sunshine," he told her. "It's happening."

MARLON HAD been no one special. Now he was building an ark. He was loved. Two years had passed. He gave the evangelical influencer a tour, and that video went viral, too. A letter for Marlon arrived at the shelter. It was from the artist Christo, whom Marlon had long admired, and it buoyed his spirits. Marlon read it aloud to Glenda in her office, gripping the divider that set her desk apart from the rest of the room. "Congratulations on the ark. I wish I had thought of it." That was it—the whole letter. His heart was pounding. He was experiencing a paroxysm of confidence. "We have to put this somewhere," he said.

"It should maybe go in the ark," Glenda said, "so that everybody can see it."

"Come with me!" Marlon said. "Let's go put it up."

"But I'm working," she said.

"This is your work!" he said. "Come on, come with me!"

Down at the shipyard, the men were caulking. Ever since the upper deck had been added, Manny, Buck, Davis, and Joe had taken to sleeping on the ark. It felt good to them to be out in the late-summer air, drinking and smoking cigarettes as they pleased, ruleless and free. They had a feeling of ownership over it that was different from Marlon's—greater than his, in their minds, though they knew they'd never get the credit. None of them had been named in any of the articles. They and their friends had been identified only as "the homeless." They all accepted this in stride, except Buck, who added it to his list of grievances against Marlon.

"Look what I got," Marlon said when he arrived. Glenda was holding the letter, and he took her hand and held it up.

Buck stood and grabbed the paper, then lowered his head over it for several seconds. Then he said, "Y'all, check it out—Marlon got a letter about the ark from Christ." His tone was mocking.

"Not Christ. Christo."

"Who in hell is that?" said Manny.

"A famous artist," Marlon said. "I don't think I would have ever dreamt this up—the Ark—if I hadn't witnessed and admired the enormous scale of Christo's ambition. Christo and da Vinci are my greatest influences."

"Never heard of any Christo," Buck muttered.

"Never heard of him! Buck! This man put six hundred thousand square meters of pink polypropylene fabric out in the middle of Biscayne Bay!"

"Never heard of polypropylene fabric, never heard of Christo, never heard of Biscayne Bay," Buck said, hotly this time, holding the letter out to Glenda with a square look.

"Okay, Buck," Glenda said quietly, taking the letter. "That's fine."

Marlon retrieved the paper from her and refolded it into thirds. He felt ashamed. He couldn't bring himself to look at Glenda. He sure as hell wasn't leaving the letter in the ark with these men. There was no telling what Buck might do with it. Marlon would bring it back to the shelter, he decided, and tape it to the wall next to Glenda's couch. On those nights that he woke up in a cold sweat, his heart pounding, unmoored from all sense of meaning, he could reach out and touch the paper and feel all right with the world.

But the next morning, when he showed up at the shipyard, Buck was gloating. He'd gone online and researched arks. It hadn't been hard to do. It turned out that other replica arks existed.

One in the Netherlands, one in Hong Kong. The one in the Netherlands housed a church, and the one in Hong Kong had a whole amusement park inside. He presented all this to Marlon with an air of great satisfaction. Marlon pretended not to care, but he cared. In truth, he hadn't known about the other arks. When he'd made his video, he hadn't thought to research that. Now he marveled at his own recklessness.

When Manny asked Marlon what this meant for them, he shrugged. He pointed out that those arks were not constructed with traditional materials and methods. That was one big difference, he said. The other was that theirs had a social purpose.

"What purpose is that?" Buck said.

"Fighting climate change," he said. He felt too ridiculous to mention the part about homelessness.

That night, at the shelter, he told Glenda what had happened. "I'm right, right?" he said.

"Right," Glenda said. But there was something in her voice.

He could tell, the air was going out of their balloon. He realized he needed to figure out what to do about it.

THEN THREE years were up. The unveiling approached. Marlon was working on his angle, his approach; his plan was to hold the gala at the shipyard itself and announce there that he needed an extra infusion of funding to, in the funders' parlance, get it over the finish line. Glenda had agreed to call the invitees herself on behalf of him and the project. Marlon had a thought. Maybe he should invite Christo to see it. He slipped the artist's name onto the list. The following afternoon, when he asked her how it had gone, she said it had gone fine. Only a couple of people had answered their phones, and they had been flattered to have gotten calls. She had left messages for the rest.

"Did you notice any special names?" he said.

"Do you mean Christo's?" she said.

At her tone, which was flat and almost annoyed, he felt ashamed. "I didn't mean anyone in particular," he said. He was beginning to dread the unveiling. It had been an essentially optimistic project, completely unlike any he had undertaken in the past. But he was not an optimist. It occurred to him that his angle, his approach, had been all wrong from the start.

"I left a message," she said.

On the eve of the unveiling, Marlon came back to their room to find Glenda in an oversized T-shirt bearing the name of her church. Her legs, bare underneath the shirt, were thin and white and hairless. He looked at her and felt sorry about it all. "Come on, put on some pants," he said.

"How come?" she said.

"Let's go to the roof," he said. "Let's get a good look at it."

Almost as soon as they opened the door to the rooftop and climbed out, it was clear something was wrong. Brownish smoke was billowing out through the open portholes. "Is that—" Glenda said.

"Fire," Marlon said, nodding. They could hear sirens approaching.

When they reached the shipyard, a crowd had gathered. They pushed through to the front and found a firefighter. "There could be men inside!" Glenda shouted over the noise. The firefighter shook his head, uncomprehending. She stood on her tiptoes and put her mouth to his ear. "Men! Inside!" The firefighter shook his head. "We looked—there's no one in there!" he shouted. Marlon could see crooked fingers of flame reaching up to the sky, bending, touching each other. The air snapped, and a hiss of sparks flew up and hung briefly in the air like stars. Hunks of wood blackened, cracked, and fell flaming to the ground. Marlon could taste the burning in his throat. His face felt seared.

"Someone needs to go in," Glenda pleaded with him.

"They're not in there, I'm sure," Marlon said. "I told them to sleep in the shelter tonight, because of the unveiling."

Glenda clutched her head. "You can't be sure! Marlon! Do something!"

She was right, he realized, that something must be done. Marlon took his phone from his pocket and began recording the fire. It was as beautiful as he had thought it would be when he dreamed it up—the great masterpiece of his life. How ridiculous he had been, at first, to believe that he, artist of the ephemeral, would build a functional ark and put it in the water. That was the part that hadn't been right from the start. The blackness—that of the pieces as they sparked and fell off—was scarier than any black he'd seen in his life, not blacker, but more frightening. It was an annihilating blackness. He could imagine himself falling into it and never coming out. "Stand there!" he shouted. "Explain what's happening! Glenda, it feels like we're standing right in the middle of hell, doesn't it?"

Glenda regarded him with an expression that made him feel as if only he were in hell and not her, as if she were looking down on him from a place of safety and grace, both pitying him and feeling glad to not be down there with him. It reminded him of all the women who had loved him, and fallen out of love with him, before her. But this, too, was beautiful. This disintegration: art.

LATER, AN investigation would conclude definitively that no men had been in there. Manny, Buck, Davis, and Joe had slept through it all, at the shelter, as Marlon had said. The cause of the fire remained a mystery, though the funders had commissioned an investigation. Marlon had filled his truck with as many chunks of the dead ark as would fit and left town. For his next installation, he would reconfigure the burned chunks of wood into a small replica of his ark, while, on a screen on one wall, the video of the conflagration played. Glenda stayed behind. She thought often—she prayed often—about what had been meant by all of this. It seemed pointless. She sat at her desk at the shelter, waiting for a signal about what to do next. God had made a promise to her, as he had to anyone who trusted in Him. She waited and received no signal. She waited and had faith.

As long as the earth endures, seedtime and harvest, cold and heat, summer and winter, day and night will never cease. The remains of the ark lay there until a contractor hired by the funders showed up to haul away the pieces. The contractor sold the good material to a lumberyard, where much of it was discovered by a newly married couple remodeling their home. The handsome beams across the ceiling of the living room were once part of the hull. The dining room table was the section of bulkhead against which Glenda and Marlon once leaned and kissed. The married couple wonder aloud about the exact provenance of their furniture. It's all recycled material, they tell their friends. It's all sustainable. They go around pointing to the items one by one. This is salvaged, this is salvaged!

You Are Not Alone

A GIRL STANDS AT baggage claim at Orlando International Airport, waiting for her father to come and get her. The girl is turning eight. She lives in Seattle with her mother, but her mother isn't feeling well, so she has been sent to stay with her father for a while. Her eighth birthday has begun; she will spend the rest of it with him.

The girl reads a comic book while she waits. Her escort, from the airline, stands next to her. Her father was supposed to come to the gate, but he didn't. The escort called his number, but he didn't pick up. The escort is a flight attendant. She seems annoyed. The girl sees her own suitcase come around the carousel, but she doesn't know what to do about it. It is too heavy for her. She watches her suitcase go around and around. After a while, she walks up to the carousel. "Tell me when you see it," the escort says. When it arrives, the girl leans forward and brushes it with her fingertips. "This is mine," she says, and she waits for her escort to help her retrieve it. The escort does.

The girl sits down on her suitcase, waiting, turning eight, reading her comic book. One by one, the adults take their own suitcases and leave. The escort doesn't ask if she's okay. She isn't that little anymore, and she is tall for her age. Adults, she tells herself, don't look at you when you're eight: too old to be cute, too young to be beautiful.

After a while, the girl feels someone moving behind her, but she is afraid to turn and look. Then, there is a pair of hands over her eyes. The fingers are thin and solid, like the twigs of a tree. These are the hands of a stranger. The girl closes her book. "Ma'am," the escort says. The stranger laughs. She has a happy laugh. "I'm her stepmother," the stranger says.

"That's enough," says a man's voice. This is her father. His rough, salt-smelling hands take the stranger's hands from the girl's eyes. Both the girl's father and the stranger come around in front of the girl.

"Daddy," she says. She hasn't seen her father since she was little.

Her father takes her in his arms and squeezes for a long time. "Hi, baby," he says. He doesn't have a mustache anymore. His top lip is too fat. The girl's chest feels tight. You're not a baby, she tells herself. When he lets go, he puts his hand on the stranger's hand. The stranger lifts that hand and clasps the girl's hand with it. They form a stack of three hands, together, like they're making an oath. The stranger is wearing a tank top and gym shorts, with a thin slice of flesh exposed at her stomach. She has light brown skin and a long face. Her eyes and mouth are big, like the features of a doll; her nose is potatoish. The stranger uses her whole face to smile. She is trying, but she is not beautiful.

"Surprise," the girl's father says, in a shy and apologetic voice.

*   *   *

THE SURPRISE, the girl supposes, is the stranger. But the girl already knows about her. A while ago, while her mother was still well, a package arrived in the mail from her father. She opened it hurriedly, looking for bills: He usually sent ten dollars. But this time there were no bills, only a fridge magnet of the Virgin Mary; a blue-and-purple silk scarf; a booklet about the teachings of Buddha; and a family photograph of a dozen people wearing white. There was a letter, too. In it, her father wrote that, ever since his divorce from her mother, he had been searching for another lady with whom he could share his hopes and dreams. Recently, he had found that lady. She was a nurse from Brazil. Her name was Yara. She was a spiritual person, a Buddhist. They had gotten married. Now they lived together, and he had told Yara to collect some items to send his daughter that would help her understand something about her father's new wife. The letter ended: "Now that I've explained all this, I feel much better!"

In the car ride to their house, the stranger sits in the backseat with her and leans her head against the window. The girl wonders, for the first time, how her father met a Brazilian nurse.

The girl's father wants to hear about what the girl has been doing with herself. He feels ashamed. He doesn't say it, but the girl can hear the shame in his voice. The girl's mother has been institutionalized. She has been institutionalized because she had a mental breakdown. She had a mental breakdown because the girl's father—a fun and charming and handsome man who nevertheless couldn't be trusted, according to her mother—had gotten a new wife.

The girl's aunt has been staying in the girl's apartment with her.

The girl talked to her mother over the phone before going to Florida. The girl wanted to visit her mother. But she couldn't, not yet.

Her father is a general contractor. The girl tells her father she has been drawing; she would like to be an artist. He glances back at her in the rearview mirror. "Oh, that's no good for a smart girl like you. Be a scientist, an engineer. You're intelligent."

"Or be a nurse," the stranger says. These are the first words she has spoken to the girl.

"Not a nurse," the girl's father says. "She's smart."

The stranger glances at her father and then turns to face the girl. "Intelligence is important, but passion is more important," she says. "When I was a girl, I was given a complicated toy, made of ramps and balls. To play with the toy well, I had to learn some basic concepts of physics. From then on, I loved physics. I taught myself more about it, and I decided to become a physicist: I wasn't a good student, but I was *passionate* about it. I fought for physics, from the age of ten, like I was fighting a great battle. But this is how it works: All the top students want to study engineering, but there are very few spots for engineering. Then, the second-most-desirable area of study is physics. So we took the examination, and all the top students took all the spots for engineering, and the students who scored well, but not at the top, took all the spots for physics. Those of us who wanted so badly to become physicists but didn't score well had to choose a different field. I went to my mother, and I said, 'Mother, I am so confused. What should I do?' My mother said, 'You are a kind person. Why not become a nurse?' I said, 'But I cannot.' I was afraid of blood at that time. She said, 'You can!' So I applied to nursing school, but still, I did not want to attend. It was far away from home, and I was attached to my home, to my sisters in particular. They were very young, and I felt responsible for them. And then there was the problem of the blood. Still, when I got in, I went, though I didn't know what to expect. On the first day, I stepped into the hospital and saw the suffering on these people's faces and felt such a connection and thought, Yes! I can do it. From then on, I found a new passion. I hardly even think of physics. That is how life is. If you have passion, you can attach that passion to anything."

THE GIRL'S father lives in a small town near the ocean. He tells the girl that when he was her age and lived nowhere near water, he told himself that he would live by the ocean as an adult. The girl's age, he tells the girl, is the best age to be. It's the first time he has mentioned her age: She was wondering if he remembered her birthday—maybe he did, after all. Childhood, everyone says, is the best time of life. Her mother was a teenager when she met her father; meeting him, her mother told her, is what destroyed her life.

On the way to her father's house, the girl sees blue-feathered peacocks roaming in the streets. She has never seen anything like it. They walk out in front of the car and cock their hips like teenagers.

"Daddy," the girl says, "look."

"Pretty, aren't they—should I stop?"

But she is afraid of them. "Don't!" she says.

He doesn't. He turns down a street, slows his car, and rolls down his windows. "This is our street," the stranger says. She taps her thin fingers along the rim of the open window. She looks to the girl. "Do you like it?" she says.

The neighbors are working on some rosebushes in their yard. They're an older couple. The man comes to the car window and claps the girl's father on the shoulder. "How goes it?" he says.

"Not bad," the girl's father says.

"Bom dia," the man says to the stranger. "Como vai?"

"Tudo bem," the stranger says.

The man says to the stranger, "You know, I told the guys at work to witness their thoughts—I said, 'My neighbor's wife says everybody should witness their thoughts'—and my coworker said, 'That's crazy. That's impossible.' Now, when I skip our morning smoke break—"

"He's trying to quit," the woman calls, from where she is standing over the rosebushes.

"She wants me to quit," the man says.

"It's his cholesterol," the woman says.

"Good, Jack, smoking is very bad for the heart," the stranger says.

"So when I skip our morning smoke break, my buddy says, 'What's the problem, Jack? You busy witnessing your thoughts?' I say, 'In fact, I witnessed my thoughts on the way to work this morning, and they—my thoughts—said, 'Jack, lay off the cigarettes, man!'"

"Ha-ha-ha," the stranger says.

"But anyway, this must be the little one!" the man says, peering into the car at the girl. "He won't stop talking about you!"

WHEN THEY get to his house, the girl goes upstairs to take a shower. Walking up the stairs, she hears her father say to the stranger, "I love you." It is a strange sound, to her, those words put together like that. She has never heard him say those words to anyone but her, and never in that romantic, full-mouthed tone. She wonders if her father used to talk to her mother like that—she wonders if that's what made her mother feel deceived by him, later, when he left.

The girl can't imagine any man loving her mother. Her mother is not that kind of person: not the kind of person you imagine a man loving. When the girl was younger and wanted to hear her mother laugh, she used to tickle her. Her mother would laugh, and the girl would feel proud of herself. Now that the girl is turnIng eight, she knows it means nothing for people to laugh when tickled.

THE STRANGER has the idea to spend the afternoon kayaking on the nearby river. The girl's father likes the idea. The girl, he says, is old enough now for her own small kayak. The three of them get on bikes and head toward the river. The girl's father calls out to the girl periodically, and when she answers, he says, "Okay?" and she says, "Okay!" She is biking behind him and in front of the stranger, and sometimes he glances back, quickly, and grins. The sun is high and hot. Sweat beads on his wide nostrils.

They near a bridge. The girl sees a boy fishing with a man, probably his father. The boy looks like he could be the girl's age. The man has a tattoo on the back of his sunburned neck: JESUS, it reads. He reaches back and scratches it with one hand, keeping the other on top of his son's hand, which grips the fishing rod. Both father and son are blond-haired. Then the fishing rod slips into the river, and the man shouts, "Christ!" and slaps the boy across the back of his head. The boy's head bows down and stays down. The girl, her father, and the stranger pass the boy and the man. The bridge cracks in half and rises to let a sailboat pass underneath.

"Damn," the girl's father says. "We missed it." His nostrils flare. They slow their bikes to a stop. They wait.

"I wish I had a bike at home," she says.

"Your mom should have gotten you a bike," the girl's father says. "She should have put you in soccer classes. She should have bought you summer clothes. The bare necessities!" The girl's father seems worked up about it.

The stranger sneezes, a big, generous sneeze; the girl says, "Bless you," and the stranger says, in a serious voice, "God bless us all." The bridge comes back down, and the three of them take off pedaling over it, to the other side of the river.

THE GIRL'S father tells her he has wanted her to visit for a long time. This time, if she likes it, she can come and live with him. Earlier, at his house, her father kept rearranging his things—the saltshaker, the books on the bookshelf—and looking at her. The girl could tell what was on his mind. He wanted to know if she wanted to come and live with him. She knows her mother doesn't want her to do that. She said so on the phone.

"Why not?" the girl said to her mother on the phone.

"Because I am your mother," her mother said.

But her father said it is up to her. Her father said she is growing up and can make grown-up decisions.

It's up to her. She will have to decide. She will have to work out the question of her father's trustworthiness.

They reach the kayak shop. The girl's father gets off his bike first, and the girl scrambles behind him, not wanting to be left alone with the stranger. The kayak man asks them to each choose one. The stranger wavers; she likes both the yellow one and the red one. She asks the girl's father to pick one for her. The girl thinks the kayaks are all the same. The girl thinks the stranger might be the kind of person who thinks differently colored M&M's taste different, even though they don't. The girl's father chooses the red kayak for the stranger and takes the yellow one himself. The girl chooses a blue one.

"You must like blue," the stranger says. "Colors have symbolic meaning. Blue signifies calm. I am a bit afraid of the water. In the newspaper the other day, they said there are alligators in this river, but they aren't dangerous."

The girl feels a prickle of fright in her cheeks and armpits. "Are there, Daddy?" the girl says. "Aren't they? Dangerous?"

"No, no," her father says with a laugh, and he puts an arm around the stranger's waist.

"In any case, your father will protect us," the stranger says. The girl's father looks at the stranger as if he will protect her. The stranger is wearing sunglasses. They are huge, with thick, red frames. Light bounces from the water where the sun reflects, and hurts the girl's eyes. The girl wants sunglasses, but her mother thinks she is too young. The girl understands what her mother is talking about. The girl likes that about sunglasses.

"I want sunglasses," the girl says, looking at the stranger.

"We'll get you some sunglasses at the mall," her father says. "You can have anything you like. You can have lots of sunglasses."

"My eyes hurt," the girl says to the stranger.

"Here," the stranger says, taking off her sunglasses. "Wear mine."

"Okay," the girl says. She puts on the sunglasses. She is surprised by the brownness of things.

The stranger laughs. "Look at her!" the stranger says. "She looks like a famous actress!"

The girl strikes a pouty pose, and they all laugh.

THE GIRL has to enter her blue kayak. She is afraid. She is turning eight and doesn't want anyone to see her afraid. She puts herself in a strong mood. She gets into her kayak and sits. It wobbles, then rights itself. The kayak man gives her a paddle. Her father and the stranger get paddles, too.

"Like this," her father says, pulling up next to her and demonstrating with his paddles. "Put some muscle into it."

She tries, and her kayak moves.

"There!" he says. "Good!"

They paddle.

After a while, the girl's father points and cries out, "A dolphin! Did you see that?"

"Where? Where?" the girl says. She didn't see.

"Ah, you missed it!" her father says. "Stop. Wait. Keeping watching. Pay attention. To be an engineer, you need to pay attention."

The three of them stop; they wait. They face one another in their kayaks, which gently drift in the current. You want to be an artist, the girl tells herself. You don't want to be an engineer.

"You know, I have a great idea," her father says. "People use telescopes to look into the sky. Why not invent a telescope that looks into the sea? We have more water in the world than anything else. Doctors can look into our stomachs. Why can't we look into the water with, you know, a little tube, with a little lens and a little light? Do you think we should register it in the patent office? We can sell it for fifty bucks. What do you think? Will you move here and be my business partner?"

The girl laughs. "That's a good idea," she says.

Her father says, "Your dad is a genius, isn't he? Don't tell anybody. Keep my secret."

"I like boats."

"I like boats, too. You take after me."

"If I move here, can we get a boat?"

"Yes, yes, absolutely!"

The river ripples around them. She wonders if he's telling the truth.

"There's a concept in physics called catastrophe theory," the stranger says. "I don't understand it well. But here's an example: If a stick is caught in the mud in a river, the pattern of ripples around it changes according to some predicable mathematical rules. But at a certain point—a moment—the rippling suddenly becomes unpredictable. That's the moment of catastrophe."

"People will sit in their boats, just like we're doing at this moment," her father says, "and they'll use their telescopes to look into the water and see all the dolphins and the fish and the sea turtles."

"Will that be allowed?" the girl says.

"Allowed by who?"

"The government?"

"Who taught you about the government? Your mother? Does she teach you that you have to follow the rules of the government of the United States of America? Ha!"

"No," the girl says. "I learned it myself. I learned it at school."

"At school. Jesus Christ."

"One day, you'll come with your father and me to visit Brazil!" the stranger interjects. "The best time to come is during Carnival, and the best place to go is to Rio de Janeiro. Your father is learning to speak Portuguese."

The stranger points to the girl's father, who is paddling next to her. He makes a face. The stranger erupts in laughter, clapping her hands. The girl doesn't understand what's funny. She wonders if the stranger will drop her paddle, but she doesn't. It somehow balances there on the sides of the kayak, even as she claps her hands and rocks with laughter. She strikes the girl as that kind of person you meet sometimes—a lucky person, a gravity-defying person.

The stranger snaps her fingers and says, "I know. Let's show her the Portuguese alphabet. A."

"Ah," says the girl's father.

"B."

"Beh."

"C."

"Seh," says the girl's father, and they go on like that. He slips up only on *J*. The stranger laughs again, and he does, too.

"We called my mother, and your father spoke to her in Portuguese," the stranger says. "She was so impressed! He said, 'Good morning,' and then he said, 'How are you?' Tomorrow I will show you photographs of my mother. That way, you will come to know your new family."

"Tell her that her English is good," the girl's father says to the girl.

"Your English is good."

"Oh no, no, you are very generous," the stranger says. "I told your father to correct me, and he did not. That is, until something very embarrassing happened. We saw a man selling fruit— right here, near this river. I said, 'Come, let's have some fruit,' and your father agreed. He paid the man, and while we stood there, I opened the banana and took one bite and said, 'Oh, this banana is so rape.' I meant to say 'ripe,' and I said, 'rape'!"

"Hey, she's only eight," the girl's father says, his nostrils flaring.

The sun has drifted lower in the sky. It is quiet on the river. In the distance, a black mass of birds comes out from behind a river bend and flocks across the sky, close to the water.

"Watch them!" says the girl's father. "To be an engineer, you have to pay attention: The people who invented airplanes studied birds to figure out how to do it."

The stranger takes a deep breath and lets it out. "Or pay

attention for no reason," she adds. "One can pay attention simply to pay attention."

The girl is paying attention.

THE NIGHT before her mother was institutionalized, the girl could hear her talking to herself. Then the girl's mother called her name, and the girl went slowly into her mother's room. The girl's mother lay in bed flat on her back, with the comforter pulled way up to her chin. Her knuckles gripped it, next to her face. Everything was angles: the corners of the room; the sharp headboard; the mother's jaw; a hanging decoration the girl had strung together for her, a mobile made out of a thousand origami cranes, which the girl had folded and built herself, for good luck. Her mother gestured at them: "Hurry, put them somewhere else! They're too loud!"

"I don't hear anything," the girl said. The birds were silent, suspended mid-flight.

"You're not *listening*," her mother said. "Move them, now."

The girl stepped in her socks onto the nightstand. Standing there, she reached up—and that's when she realized her mother was right. She listened, and she heard it: the sly, papery rustle of the birds' wings. Swiftly, she slipped them from the hook on which they hung, hopped down, and ran with them from the room, down the hall, and into her room. All this time, they rustled even more loudly and brushed against her. In her room, the girl stood there, and the birds quieted. She flung the birds into her closet and slammed the door. For a split second, they kept up their thrashing, as if they were flying up against the door and trying to get out. Then they were still. She felt proud for having helped her mother.

But in the middle of the night, the girl found her aunt sleeping in her mother's bed. The girl's mother was gone.

"OKAY," SAYS the stranger. "Let's keep moving."

"Let's move," the girl's father says.

The girl wants to be alone for a while. She takes off ahead of her father and the stranger. Soon they are far behind her, paddling slowly next to each other. People talk about rivers as if they're blue, but they're not: They're dark, greenish-black. The girl's paddle stirs up algae. She looks back. Her father and the stranger are far behind, paddling side by side. When the girl looks ahead again, she sees a dark shape emerge from the water, then duck back down. She looks toward the spot where the form emerged. It ripples and bubbles.

"Daddy?" the girl says quietly. Her father and the stranger are far behind, and they don't hear her. The girl stops her kayak and waits. She looks at that spot ahead of her, and the dark form comes up again. It looks like a submerged rock, at first, but then she sees a pair of wet, bulbous eyes over broad nostrils. This is what an alligator looks like, she thinks, and she is afraid. The alligator stares at her. Its eyes and nose look angry. The girl stares back. The alligator slowly ducks its head underwater. Don't move, she tells herself. That, it seems, is the important thing. Don't move.

After some time, the stranger pulls up next to the girl. "Are you okay?" the stranger says. "You have a very serious expression."

"I'm fine, thank you," the girl says, still looking at that spot. "Where is my dad?"

The stranger says the girl's father has asked her to take the girl to the island up ahead, where they will tie up their kayaks and eat a picnic of fruit and bread.

"Let's wait for him, and we can all go," the girl says.

"He said he'd meet us there," the stranger says. "He wants us to get to know each other a little bit."

"I want to wait here," the girl says.

"Come on," the stranger says, smiling. "We'll have a nice talk." The stranger paddles ahead, slowly, and soon she is near the spot where the girl saw the alligator. The girl doesn't say anything. She wonders what will happen. If something happens to the stranger, she thinks, it won't be her fault. She is sure something will happen. The spot is still rippling. The stranger keeps paddling, and when she gets to the spot where the girl saw the alligator, she turns and says, still smiling, "Come on!" The stranger is just sitting there in the alligator spot, waiting, the river rippling and bubbling around her.

So the girl takes up her paddle and rows toward the stranger. Her hands are shaking, and she worries about dropping the paddle. The girl could use the telescope that her father hasn't invented yet. When she gets to the alligator spot, she is sure something will happen. It doesn't. The girl and the stranger sit there for a second in their kayaks, and then row in silence toward the island.

The stranger looks occasionally at the girl.

"Okay?" the stranger says.

"I'm fine, thank you, ma'am," the girl says. She says that—*ma'am*—to hurt the stranger's feelings.

At the island, the stranger steps from her kayak to the small dock and ties her boat to it. The stranger puts out a hand toward the girl, who also has her kayak next to the dock. The girl looks at the dock. It is right next to her kayak. She stands gently, rocking her feet to stay steady. She stays steady. She looks at the dock. The stranger is standing there with her hand out. The girl jumps to the dock without help. She ties up her own kayak. She takes off the stranger's sunglasses and gives them back to the stranger. Things look bright again.

"You can keep them," the stranger says, sitting down on the dock next to the boats.

The girl stands there. "I don't like your sunglasses," the girl says. "I don't like the brown look of things."

The stranger seems unbothered. "Come, sit," she says. "Your father wants us to get to know each other a little bit. He said, 'Give her a bit of motherly advice.' I said, 'She is mature for her age. I don't know what I can tell her that she doesn't already understand.' I thought for a long time about what I could tell you. Then it came to me. I can teach her about meditation, I thought. I can teach her to witness her thoughts."

The girl is afraid. She sits next to the stranger but tries not to touch her.

"The word *yoga* means union," the stranger says. "You ask, union between what and what? I'll tell you. Union between self and self. See this river?"

The girl sees the river. There are ripples all over its surface. The stranger gets up and walks up the dock, toward the shore. The girl doesn't know if the stranger wants her to follow. She stays put. The stranger squats on the ground, raking her fingers through it. She gets up and jogs back. She crouches and holds her fist out to the girl, then opens it. There are several pebbles in it. The girl doesn't understand. She doesn't know if the stranger wants her to take a pebble. She doesn't. The stranger takes a pebble with her other hand and tosses it in the river.

"Your mind is like this river," the stranger says. "Your thoughts are these pebbles, which cause ripples in the water." She is tossing pebbles into the river as she speaks. "You must clear your mind so that it is like this river. You must witness your thoughts and let them go." She stops talking. She stops throwing pebbles. But the river is still rippling. It has nothing to do with the pebbles: Those ripples were there from the start. The stranger looks ahead with a serene expression. The girl doesn't see anything familiar in this expression. She feels all alone.

"You want me to do that?" the girl says.

"Yes," the stranger says.

"I have to do it now?" the girl says.

"Yes," the stranger says.

Her father's kayak is far away. The girl closes her eyes.

"Keep your eyes open," the stranger says. "Sit up straight."

The girl does as the stranger says.

"Witness your thoughts," the stranger says. "Witness your thoughts."

You are not alone, the girl is thinking. I—your self—am here.

The girl is thinking of the boy she saw fishing; she is thinking of catching a fish, of taking hold of it and letting it beat itself to death in her hand. Maybe if she stays, he will get her a fishing rod. Everything she has said she wants, he has said he will give her. That tells her nothing about his trustworthiness or untrustworthiness. She won't be sure until he gives it to her, but he won't give it to her unless she stays. It's an impossible situation. But then, it's her birthday. Whether he remembers and gives her a gift—that will be a clue, at least.

There he is, coming closer in his kayak. Her father, seeing his daughter with his beloved, is thinking, I hope they're getting to know each other a little bit. He's thinking, This is your one chance to win her over; don't mess it up like you've messed up everything else in life; don't let her go back to her crazy mother or else the craziness might seep into her. These things are passed down through genes but they can be kept from expressing themselves if you nurture a child right. A bicycle, a kayak: She should have some small things of her own, she should have some delight in her life, a child shouldn't be so fearful all the time. He sees a dolphin leap from the water up ahead, and he thinks, Beautiful! Beautiful! I wish she could have seen that: beautiful!

His beloved waves at him, then looks at the girl. O que ela está pensando? she thinks. She feels terrible for mentioning rape to the girl. She did it out of nervousness and because English isn't her first language. She will have to learn how to speak to a young girl in a language that isn't her own, she will have to learn motherhood. The girl still seems like a stranger to her, like a child you might pass on the street without giving her a thought besides noticing that her hair clip is charming, for example, or that her voice is irritatingly glum. She thinks of her own mother and misses her and wonders if she made the right decision, leaving her own family behind. Trying to create a new existence for herself at this age—like playacting. It feels as if she's in a film sometimes, a foreign one, in English, and the subtitles are turned off. When her father was dying, she could not return to see him in time; he tried to hold on for her—her sisters told her later—but by the time her plane landed, he was gone. Her mother visited her in Florida afterward. She was supposed to stay for six months, but she didn't even fully unpack and left after three weeks, because she couldn't handle the isolation of life in the United States; the emptiness of the streetscapes didn't suit her, não há ninguém aqui. She could not explain to her mother—it would have been unfair—that she needed her. While everyone believed she wanted to care for her mother in her grief, it had only been partly about that, it was also, it was mostly, that she needed her mother, she was lonesome, too. But she could not explain that part; she was not a girl anymore, she had not been one for a long time, though on some level—she wanted to tell the girl—we feel like girls for all our lives, even after we choose careers, get married, it's all playacting.

"It is not possible to reason our way to true understanding," she says. "Life is so deep it cannot be understood. There is a word for this in my language: *incompreensível*."

"*Incomprehensible*," the girl tells her.

"We must witness our thoughts, and then let them go," she says.

"I did," the girl says, "then I did."

Unknown Unknowns

TOLD OUR SON I had something to tell him that would blow his mind: By the time he's old enough to drive, I said, there wouldn't be such a thing as driving anymore. Cars, I said, would drive themselves. I really thought he'd find that exciting. He was four and loved inventions. But he found it boring. Autonomous vehicles, he said, as if the phrase were a punch line. Our driverless future, he said. This was several years ago. My God, we didn't know the half of it yet—that, before long, the world's richest man would be mining space for trillion-dollar asteroids, would be dotting the night sky with internet satellites, would be hatching a plan to leave this planet behind and colonize another, that the universe didn't stand a chance against such progress. Back then, all seemed salvageable yet. That afternoon, our son got my husband to promise to save our car for him. The next morning, he got my mom to do the same. But what are you going to do with two old cars, I said, in our driverless future? I'm going to drive them, of course, he said. I'm going to drive them across the world. What about the ocean? I said. What about it? he said. Do you know about the United Arab Emirates? Do you believe in the Burj Khalifa?

THE QUESTION of belief—of the gap between knowing and not knowing—interested him. Do you believe in Santa Claus? he asked. To hedge, I said I wasn't sure one way or another. He told me he had two questions to help me think through it. Have you ever woken up on Christmas morning, he said, and seen a huge pile of presents? I told him I had—what about them? Ask yourself, he said. Who put them there? Also, have you ever seen an old man with a long white beard? I told him I had. Ask yourself, he said. Who is that man?

THAT MAN was Bernie, who was upset with someone. That one was Joe, who looked like a good grandfather. That woman was Kamala, who looked like me, and that other man was Julian, who looked like him—but they didn't stand a chance. The colors Elizabeth wore were wrong—the fact that she wore colors at all, and not black, like the others. Pete? Who is Pete? Who is that man? It didn't matter who won this round, he said, because Donald Trump would beat that person in the next one, no matter what. I love Donald Trump, he said. I love villains. Come on, I said. Guns, he said. Come on, I said. Guns, he said. Guns, guns, guns—fire.

* * *

FIRE INTERESTED him. My husband and I were worried, how-
ever, about using our fireplace. It was the first house we'd had
with a fireplace. It wasn't about the fire. It was the question of
how to know whether the gas valve was open or closed. We knew
it was closed at the time, but if we opened it, we might forget
which way was open and which way was closed, which seemed
dangerous, so, in those four years of our son's life, none of us had
ever seen the fireplace lit. Come on, our son said. In Mongolia,
people build fires right in the middle of their huts. It's a source
of heat and a source of light. I didn't know that, I said. He was
learning, at school, about human progress. Mongolian yurts. The
Burj Khalifa. There are known knowns, as Donald Rumsfeld
said; there are things we know we know. We also know there are
known unknowns; that is to say, we know there are some things
we do not know.

BUT THERE are also unknown unknowns, as that man said—the
ones we don't know we don't know. One morning, I awoke to the
sound of our son singing out from his bedroom, Let it go, let it
go, can't hold it back anymore, as was his wont, and when I went
downstairs and opened his door, he sat up and said he had something to tell me that would blow my mind. In the middle of the
night, he had awoken to a flash of light outside. He thought for a
moment that it was morning. He climbed out of bed and onto the
rocking chair, looked out the window for the source of light, and
there he saw something really amazing: a train of bright little dots
arcing soundlessly across the sky one right after the other, maybe
fifty of them, and then disappearing over the horizon. Not stars.
Not fireflies. Not airplanes. He waited to see what would happen

next, but nothing did, so he returned to bed and slept. So what were they? he said, his eyes glinting, as if it were a riddle. I don't know—what were they? I said, feeling he had some answer in mind. I don't know—what were they? he said. But I don't know— what were they? Ask yourself. Who put them there?

The Hormone Hypothesis

I FEEL BADLY FOR my husband—for men in general—because they're left out of so much of human life. It's more common to talk about the ways in which they have it better—and God knows those abound, I'm not dismissing them—but recently I've been thinking about the ways in which they don't. We all understand, more or less, how a man's body and mind function. But I believe a man can live an entire life in this world and know nothing about the warm, vaginal smell of a women's restroom stall after someone else has used it—how it's repulsive yet also inspires a weird fellow feeling, a sense of intimacy. They know we tweeze our eyebrows, but they don't realize that many of us have nipple hairs that we also tweeze out—they can grow long, it's impressive, half a thumb's length or more. My best friend and I used to compare our longest ones and marvel. I've seen clips online of these machines they've made that men can strap on to feel what it's like to have terrible period cramps, but that seems crude to me, unless they make a machine that can also approximate the emotional malaise.

Years ago, when I was pregnant and living in California, some older female friends—professors at the university where I got my doctorate—explained that, after childbirth, my vagina would bleed for days. I would have to wear pads in my underwear and, when I peed, use a bottle to squirt water onto my crotch to sanitize it. Given the fragility of the postpartum crotch, I would also be given a stool softener, to make my poop come out more gently, and maybe a laxative, too. This worried me.

I was also worried—I told them—that I wouldn't love my child. On internet forums, I'd read a lot of women's posts about loving their child while they were still in the womb, and I felt nothing like that, I felt only a lump expanding and hardening inside me. One of the professors, Whei, my former adviser, said she didn't love her daughter while pregnant, either, and didn't even love her much when she first came out. She seemed like a total stranger, an alien. Whei's love developed only as her daughter grew older—in fact, developed in proportion to her daughter's age, such that her love for her daughter, now eleven, was greater than it had ever been.

After Anand arrived, I remembered Whei's comments. He lost weight after being born. I was taking too long to begin lactating, and Anand didn't seem to like the taste of the formula we tried feeding him instead. He would bawl at the sight of the bottle. On the third evening, I was sitting in a rocking chair trying, and failing again, to nurse him. I really had to use the bathroom— the stool softener, the laxative—but I didn't want to put the baby down, and I hadn't yet figured out I could just bring him with me to the toilet. So I stayed put and eventually realized I was pooping my pants. I called for my husband in a panic, handed him our bawling infant, and ran, bowlegged, to the toilet. That night, my husband began tearing up—"I'm scared that something's wrong—I just love him so much!" he said. I was scared, too, but *of* Anand, almost as if he were someone else's child who had been forced upon me. Feeling this way worried me, but knowing that Whei had felt a version of it, too, made me feel better.

It's menopause that has me thinking about all of this—or rather, perimenopause. Until recently, I didn't even know the term. I learned of it only when a couple of my friends—in Eugene, Oregon, where we'd been living—started experiencing it. None of them understood what it was at first. All three thought they were going through a midlife crisis, a breakdown of form and spirit. When they tried to go to bed at night, they'd squirm in the sheets, unable to find comfort, or else they'd fall asleep fine only to awaken feverish and filmed in sweat. It felt connected to a spiritual unsettling. One of them, Darienne, a high school teacher, confided that she was contemplating quitting and starting over as a pastor. The second, Wathana, wanted to get divorced and move to London, where she'd studied abroad in college and met her first love. The third, Clarisse, still loved her career—she was a wildlife biologist—and had no interest in physically uprooting herself. She seemed happiest of the three. But for the first time in her life, at the age of forty-six, she was experiencing baby fever. She and her wife had chosen not to have children. They had met relatively late, when most of their friends' children were already school-age, and the prospect of starting from scratch, having to find a sperm donor or adopt, exhausted them. Now she found herself swooning into every stroller that she passed in the park, radiating want. But she knew it was probably too late.

Darienne was the one who figured out what was going on with all of them, through her gynecologist, and she told the others. They went to their own doctors, who stopped short of positive diagnoses but generally supported the shared hypothesis. The

problem with perimenopause is that there's no test to determine
its onset—it's identifiable only later on, when your periods start
coming several months apart. Later, on our text thread, Clarisse sent a link to an academic article she'd come across, noting
that women in their forties commit suicide more than those in
any other age group, and an underappreciated culprit might be
perimenopause itself. Darienne sent an exploding-head emoji,
Wathana a skull. I sent four sparkle emojis; I was being sarcastic,
and I also felt like it would be false of me, not being perimeno-
pausal yet, to have as intense a reaction as the others.

But that was several years ago. Now I'm in it myself—skull
emoji—or, at least, I believe I might be. It started when we moved
to Iowa City. My husband had gotten a teaching position here.
We both earned doctorates in cultural anthropology, but while
he went into teaching, I consult on films, mostly documentaries.
I had high cholesterol for the first time in my life—an established sign—and I'd been weighed down lately by an unname-
able regret I'd never experienced before. Iowa City's summers
are hot, and climate change has recently made them worse. One
afternoon, the three of us tried to go strolling downtown, but
the heat was insufferable. Anand was about to start kindergarten. He grabbed my dress in his fist, trying to get my attention—
something he does all the time, I don't mind—and I suddenly
felt as if my personal space had been completely annihilated.
"Stop touching me!" I snapped.

Passersby gaped. I felt awful for being irritable. I apologized to
him, but I couldn't move on, I couldn't stop thinking about it. It
felt linked to the regret I'd been experiencing, though I couldn't
understand quite what one had to do with the other.

Perimenopause, I thought. My husband was skeptical. He
thought the high cholesterol was from the habit I'd recently

developed, of cooking Indian breakfast: dosa, pesarattu, upma. Previously I'd eaten fruit and yogurt. He thought I had been irritable with Anand because of the heat and because, since moving, we had been spending all our time with our son, with no preschool and no friends to call for playdates. He also pointed out that I've felt a similar spiritual foreclosing each time we've made a big change in life, I felt it when we married and again when we became parents. I said—with some irritation—that this was different. I told him about Darienne, Wathana, and Clarisse. He said their experiences had nothing to do with mine.

But I thought they did. I hate to suggest that a characteristic is the exclusive domain of one particular sex, but I believe women experience life more communally than men do. We arrive at the answers to life's questions together. Maybe it's because we have higher levels of oxytocin, the bonding hormone. When one woman asks another, before heading out for a walk together, "Should I wear sneakers or sandals?" the second recognizes it as a legitimate question, one meant to integrate both women's consciousnesses in figuring out an answer. But when I ask my husband a question like this, he'll respond, "I mean, wear sneakers if you think sneakers make more sense, and wear sandals if you want to wear sandals." If I press him—asking, for example, "Well, what kind of shoes are you wearing?"—he'll answer but will add that his own decision should have no bearing on mine.

I didn't mention all of this to my husband. I'd told him about the hypothesis before. Now I said only that I missed our friends. He said he missed them, too. He hoped we would befriend some of the colleagues he'd met while interviewing—another anthropologist and her economist husband, a sociologist, a couple in the African American Studies department. He also suggested that I meet people online in those Facebook groups for newcomers or parents. Normally I would resist that—it irritated me, the thought of ordering up a friend online—but I did join, and one morning, in the parents' group, I noticed a post from someone named Fernanda. She looked close to my age—in her forties. By then, kindergarten had begun, and I was at home alone all day, on Zoom meetings, while my husband went to campus. Fernanda had written about having recently moved with her family to Iowa City, to be closer to her sister. She hoped to find a friend with whom to check out the Colombian café that had opened near campus.

WE MET the next morning at the café. Fernanda wore a ribbed tank top—what we used to call a wife-beater—and had a detailed tattoo of a cross on her bicep. But she wasn't as tough-looking as that makes her seem; she had a soft-featured face and immediately launched into chatting, her face close to mine, as if we were already friends. She said, "I'm glad we came, it's really pretty, with the decorations, isn't it?" Plastic greenery and flowers hung from the ceiling and sprouted from centerpieces on the tables, but it wasn't kitschy, it was well arranged and festive.

"I didn't know about this place," I said.

They had just arrived from Nashville, she said—that past weekend.

"We also arrived not long ago—a month ago," I said. "It's different here, it's not like the Northwest, where I'm from. There's lots of vegetation in the Northwest."

"Colombia, where I'm from, is like that," she said. "It's supergreen there."

"But the river's good," I said. "I'm glad there's a river. Someone told me that if you go north, almost to Minneapolis, you can go rafting."

"I want to try rafting!"

"Me, too!" I said—and the promise hung in the air, that maybe, if we became friends, we could go rafting together.

We ordered coffees and churros.

I asked where she was living. She wrinkled her nose, shook her head. "It's terrible," she said. "It's one of those buildings that looks like this"—with her hands, she made the shape of a box. "It's all brick. There's a courtyard, but the grass is yellowed and flat, it doesn't feel inviting, even Isabella—our daughter—doesn't want to play on the playground there, she said it frightens her, though when I asked her what about it was frightening, she couldn't explain."

I said we were living in an apartment complex, too, and that I hated ours as well. Everyone kept their blinds down, and it gave the impression no one else lived there. "There's a pool, though—you should bring Isabella, she can swim with Anand, they'll have fun," I said.

"I wish we had a pool," she said. The problem was that her sister—who had chosen the apartment for them—had been too selective for too long. She had gone to see some apartments before this one and rejected them for various reasons—too dark, too small of a kitchen, too noisy. She selected this one, in the end, despite its flat character and sad courtyard, because they had to settle on something before school began. "We have an expression in Colombia," she said, "that the longer you take to choose, the worse it turns out."

She and her husband—Alejo was his name—had recently gone through a traumatic experience. Afterward, Nashville felt claustrophobic to them. They decided to each make a list of the top ten places in the world they wanted to live, and then choose the one they were both excited about. But when they showed each other their lists, none of their cities matched. In the end, they settled on Iowa City, where her sister lived, because it was a place they could both live with. They thought it would be good for Isabella to be near her cousins, who are close to her age, and Alejo could get work at the company where her sister works—they make farm equipment, and Alejo has relevant experience, having worked with cars. Fernanda doesn't work; she worked a lot when she was younger, but now she's a stay-at-home mom. "Americans are obsessed with being productive and earning, they believe you're not 'contributing' if you're not working, but I just want to exist. I don't mind existing."

I told her I needed to learn from her. I explained that I feel anxious if I'm not working—I work a lot. She asked what I do, and I told her about the documentaries—about how I might travel for a week at a time to, say, the Galápalagos or the Maldives, to help filmmakers shoot their documentaries in an accurate and sensitive way.

She laughed. "We're not talking about the same thing, then," she said. "I'm talking about regular work—*work*—like fixing cars, building farm machines, harvesting fruit, taking care of babies or old people. *Work*." She said that's what she got tired of. She wants to be happy—that's all she's trying to do in life, to manage to be happy—and she's found that she feels most happy when she's caring for her daughter, her husband, their small life together. They're poorer because of it, but she and her husband feel it's worth it. "That must sound so simple, I must sound so dumb," she said.

I said it didn't; she didn't.

Our coffees and churros arrived. I asked if she and her sister were close. They didn't get along during their twenties, she said, but now they're close. I asked what happened to bring them closer. She said that, in general, they're super-different. She has a temper—Fernanda's sister. She's also a lesbian and a hardcore feminist. On the spectrum of feminism, Fernanda herself is half-feminist, but her sister is really hardcore. She believes that the patriarchy forces us to shave our legs, while Fernanda believes that she shaves her legs because she feels like it. Alejo told Fernanda, when they were still dating, that he wanted a wife who would stay home with their children, and she said—because for her it was true—that she wanted the same. But when her sister sees her washing the clothes, cooking, putting Isa to bed every night, she criticizes her for not sticking up for herself. She—Fernanda—looked at me and said we don't know each other well, she doesn't know how I feel. I wondered, privately, whether I was a half-feminist or a hardcore one. I'd like to consider myself to be on the most feminist end of the feminism spectrum. I work—I work a lot. My husband and I spend equal time with Anand. But then, I shave my legs and don't feel conflicted about it.

I shrugged; "I shave my legs," I said.

"Okay, my sister would say the patriarchy made you do it," she said. "She reads a lot, she thinks a lot—she tells me I don't think enough. For me, I don't want to think too much. If you think too much, you can't exist—the world is difficult; you can't think about that all the time, or you can't exist."

Fernanda and her sister grew closer—Fernanda said—when the situation happened. She said it like that—*the situation happened.* I said her sister must have been supportive then. She said it wasn't quite that. Her sister experienced a loss, too, it was something they went through together, and that's what made them close. Afterward, her sister realized that she might lose Fernanda as well. She insisted to Fernanda that she must hold on, she must live.

I thought she was waiting for me to ask what happened—she had brought it up twice by that point. But I hesitated, and

Fernanda continued. She said her sister is married to a woman she's been with for decades.

They met in Colombia at the age of nineteen. Fernanda's sister-in-law-to-be was backpacking there and went into a bar where Fernanda's sister was working at the time as a bartender. "Do you see all this?" Fernanda said, gesturing at her tattoos. "This is what my sister looks like—but she's got more than me, she's really butch. I used to admire her so much when I was a teenager—she's one year older than me—so when she started getting tattoos, when she cut her hair short, I copied her. I didn't understand that she was doing it because she was a lesbian."

The eighties and nineties were a turbulent time in Colombia, she said, so, growing up there, she and her sister never met foreigners. The only one they knew was a Frenchwoman married to a Colombian man, who was a client of Fernanda's mother, a seamstress. Fernanda's mother had grown up in a family descended from great wealth, but they themselves weren't rich. The maternal line had lost its wealth when Fernanda's grandmother had fallen for someone her parents didn't approve of. "He was a doctor, but he was Black," she said. "I mean, I shouldn't say 'but,' I don't mean it like that, I mean that, for that time, it wasn't common. She was white, and he was Black." When they started having children, Fernanda's grandfather decided that only the first child belonged to him, the rest belonged to the church—that is, he wouldn't support any of the children after the first one. That left five of them in all, including Fernanda's mother, who he ignored. Though her husband was a doctor, Fernanda's grandmother had to work as well to support them, and she ended up becoming a seamstress, which was how Fernanda's mother learned the trade.

Fernanda's mother—the youngest of the children—wanted to go to college, but then she met Fernanda's father. They decided she would work as a seamstress to help put him through college. He was studying environmental engineering, he wanted to work with trees. But then he became abusive. He also decided he didn't want to work in the forest after all, he wanted—Fernanda smiled darkly—to dig for gold. He left them and moved to the forest to try to find gold, and there he met and fell in love with a seventeen-year-old girl.

When she learned of his affair, Fernanda's mother filed for divorce, a big deal at that time. She was ostracized by the other mothers at Fernanda's school—she was not only divorced but was Black, a double fault. "I don't know if you're familiar with Colombia, but it's really racist there," she said. "There's racism in the U.S., but it's different—in Colombia, it's worse. Or maybe not worse, but different."

I told her that I'd been to Colombia once—to Medellín.

"Medellín—that's where I'm from!" she said. "What did you think of it?"

I told her the truth—that it was much more beautiful than I'd expected. I'd heard only of drugs and guns and jungles. But Medellín sits in a valley surrounded by big rolling hills covered with tropical trees and flowers. I explained that I was an anthropologist and had been in Medellín advising on a TV show about poor and working-class people around the world, in occupations that have been newly created by globalization.

"My God, an anthropologist," she said. "You must be really intelligent—and here I am talking and talking and talking like an idiot."

She didn't seem like an idiot. She came across as intelligent, attuned to the subtle workings of the world, an essential but ineffable quality in my field. I wondered whether she actually believed she wasn't intelligent.

I told her about my time in Medellín. I had been helping with a television series about off-the-beaten-path tourism, scouting for people to interview in a neighborhood called Comuna 13—a place that used to be violent but has since turned into a destination of sorts, with graffiti tours and shops selling Comuna 13 magnets. For the episode, we featured a tour guide who had been raped at gunpoint at the age of twelve. Her parents opposed abortion, so she had the child, and that child—the fact that she loved her and needed to keep her alive—saved her. She believed her daughter had been a miracle sent from God. "Next to Him, we are like mindless little frogs," she said. From my training, I knew not to question out loud the implication that her rape had been an act of God. "It's impossible to understand the life He has given us," she said. "He hears us praying, and it sounds to Him like, *croac, croac, croac.*"

I love talking to people who believe in God. I love their perspective, it sounds like a poem to me, their religious language. I admire their willing submission to that which is most mysterious in life. I told Fernanda this.

While Fernanda's mother struggled to pay the bills and look after her two daughters, her father lived near the gold mine with his new wife and children. He would forget Fernanda and her sister's birthdays all the time; at Christmas, he would call and tell them, "I'll be there soon!" and then wouldn't show up. Fernanda spent her whole childhood waiting for him, and then, at the age of sixteen, stopped waiting. "But what were we talking about before that?" she said.

I said she'd been telling me about meeting foreigners.

"Right," she said. The second foreigner was Helen—her sister's wife. Helen's visit was in the nineties, after the government decided they needed to make Colombia more inviting to foreigners— tourists, like Helen, but also businesses. Soon Americans started being sent by their companies to open up Colombian branches. Fernanda met one of the first to arrive—not long after her sister met Helen—and fell in love. He was forty-three; she was eighteen. She thought her father had been a pervert for marrying a teenager—but her sister had recently fallen in love with Helen, and Fernanda had been feeling lonesome and envious.

I asked if he spoke Spanish.

"A little, not much, but he had a translator," she said. "We communicated through her."

"You fell in love by communicating through a translator!" I said, interested in understanding how such a thing could happen—the logistics of it, the practicalities.

She fixed me with a worldly look—it reminded me of a look my older sister might have given me, in middle school, when explaining how romance actually functions. "I fell in love because I thought he was *handsome*," she said. "This will sound racist, but he was *so white*—and his eyes were blue, and his hair was light blond; no one's hair looks like that in Colombia." He treated her super-well, too, buying her all kinds of expensive gifts; she'd never experienced anything like it. "Imagine if an alien landed on earth, and he was so special and unusual, and he chose you," she said. "It was like that—I had my own alien."

When he had to leave Colombia and return to the U.S., he proposed marriage, so that she could go with him. She asked if I'd read a certain children's book about the mouse and the stone.

I said I hadn't heard of it.

She seemed surprised. "Oh, you have to read it, it's by a famous author—but now Anand is too old for those books," she said.

In the book, she said, a mouse who lives on an island finds a big, unusual stone. He brings it to the other mice, and they decide—because he found such a special stone—to name him king of the mice. One day, the mice are going for a walk on the island, and they round a corner, and they find a beach full of stones that look exactly like the one that the first mouse found. Then the first mouse's stone—and the first mouse himself—become ordinary again.

"You were the mouse," I said.

"I was the mouse!" she said. "I moved to the U.S. and looked around, and I realized my American wasn't special—he wasn't bad-looking, but he was average; a lot of people were pale, blue-eyed, and blond, and many of them were handsomer than him. He was a normal stone." At first she still loved him. But over time—not only because he wasn't special, but also because he got stressed at work and started to drink too much, first one margarita each night, then two, then three—she started to have doubts. On top of that, before they'd married, he'd said he didn't want children, and she agreed—but now, after marriage, having reached her mid-twenties, she realized that she did want children after all, she wanted three or four. He said he would do it under duress, but they would have to give up their carefree lifestyle, and he would resent her for the rest of their married lives. That was when she decided to divorce him. A couple of years later, she met Alejo and, poof, suddenly had a whole new life.

She abruptly flung out a hand as she said this—she gestured a lot in general—and knocked her coffee over; it spilled onto the table. We cleaned it up with napkins from the dispenser. The incident broke our conversational spell. I looked at my phone—a couple of hours had passed. Fernanda asked for the check and took it; "you can pay next time," she said, and I thanked her and agreed. But after paying, she lingered, as if she wanted to talk more.

I asked, then, if Isabella was an only child.

She said yes, but she blanched a little as she said it, and I recognized the expression, I'd seen my mom make it when some-one asked if I was her only child and she was deciding whether to explain that she'd had another daughter, who had died.

Before Isabella—Fernanda said—she and Alejo had another daughter, but she had died at only three months old, of sudden infant death syndrome. Fernanda had been the one to find her, in the morning.

Afterward, she wanted to die; she made herself stay alive only for the sake of her mother and her sister and, of course, Alejo.

"I'm Catholic," she said, a bit self-consciously. "I know there are a lot of problems with the Catholic Church—but I grew up Catholic, and I still believe in it."

"That must have helped you a lot when that happened—the situation," I said.

She said it was complicated. She still believed, she said, because she had to believe. If she didn't believe, it would be intolerable— she would have to accept that she wouldn't see her daughter in Heaven—therefore she had to believe. I said I could understand that. I thought—but didn't tell her—about how, because I don't believe, I have to accept that my sister is not in Heaven, that I won't see her again.

I told her that I understood loss, that my sister died when we were young. I said this for several reasons. First, she had been so candid, and I felt I should be as well. Second, as I mentioned, I had been reminded of my mom when she paused before telling me about her other daughter. And third, having grown up with a sister who was my guide in this life, and then having lost her, made me feel acutely the loneliness of being an only child. My entire life since, I'd been traversing the world searching for sister-shaped people to fill the space she had left. Here I was, before this relative stranger, doing it again. I didn't say all this out loud,

I only mentioned my sister's death, but I could quickly tell, from her expression, that she didn't feel that it was at all comparable to her loss. She was right. I added that I didn't mean to suggest it was similar, that it was a completely different experience.

And, to return to the topic at hand, I asked if Isa knows about her sister. She said yes—there are photos of her in the house, and they celebrate her birthday and visit the place where she's buried. It's better to talk about all this, she said, not to keep it repressed. But it's possible to remember too much—that, too, is true. They left Nashville because they couldn't bear all the reminders. "I don't know if you're like this," she said, "but, for me, when I had her, I imagined the life she would have, I pictured her growing up and going to the aquarium, playing at the playground—"

"—and when you saw other children—"

"—no, that still happens—when I see an eight-year-old girl, I think, That's the age she would have been. I mean that we couldn't stay there and keep seeing those *places*. That's why we came here. But I'm not sure that it's helping. Not yet."

"And have you thought about maybe—"

"Oh God, no, no, I can't, I've thought about it—but I'm forty-five, and I'm reaching perimenopause—"

I nodded. "Me, too, and it feels like—"

"Time ran out?"

We sat in silence for a moment. Then she stood, and I did the same, and we went together out of the café and toward our cars.

"Men, in their forties, are in their prime," I said as we walked. "It's not fair."

"Oh, but it's hard for them, too," she replied forcefully. "It's worse for them."

I laughed.

"No, really, it is," she said. "I feel badly for them—for men."

When their first daughter died, their female friends consoled Fernanda by allowing her to talk about her daughter—and her grief—all the time. But when Alejo went out with their male friends, they only joked and discussed sports and other superficialities, and when Alejo brought up their daughter, the others changed the subject.

She said that men experience the same feelings—woe, misery, terror—but are not allowed to share them, whereas women gain strength from sharing ourselves; it's what allows us to keep living despite all that we suffer—knowing that we're living it together.

"I'll give you an example," she said. She said her mom had little in common with Alejo's mom—Alejo's mother was rich and conservative, and Fernanda's poor and open-minded—but they both were ahead of their time in adventurousness. Once, on a joint family vacation, they had all rented a boat and taken it to a secluded area near lots of small islands. Everyone had been squabbling, but the water was cool and clear, and Fernanda's mother suggested they swim to one of the islands. The island wasn't that close, it would be a significant swim. Fernanda's mother-in-law agreed immediately. All the younger people—Fernanda and her husband, her sister and her wife, her sister-in-law and her husband—jumped in along with the matriarchs.

Quite quickly, Fernanda's mother-in-law took the lead. She was really fit, despite her age and having had three bouts with cancer. In her elder years, she had become a fitness buff. She swam far ahead of the rest of them, toward the island—a small, inviting island, with palm trees—but then, suddenly, she stopped in the water and started waving her arms to get their attention. Fernanda thought she was drowning. Her mother-in-law had put her palms together and was pantomiming something. She was shouting, too, but they couldn't hear her. Then they realized what she was saying: "Rayas, rayas, cuidado"—stingrays, stingrays, careful. They shouted back, "Okay," gave her the thumbs-up, and continued, but before long, they understand what she had been talking about—there weren't just a few stingrays, there was a blanket of them below, so thick you couldn't even see past them to the sea below. "We should return, all of us," Alejo said, and Fernanda agreed. They tried to call Fernanda's mother-in-law back, but she said she was fine, she was going to continue on to the island, they could pick her up there in the boat.

Then, to their surprise, Fernanda's mother said she would continue on as well. Fernanda begged her not to. It was incredibly dangerous, she said, and Alejo's mother was more fit. But her mother turned to her with a challenging air, one of intense confidence: "I might not go to the gym, but my body has been working for my whole life—I'm as strong as anyone," she said. Fernanda was shocked—she couldn't respond. Her mother took off and caught up with her mother-in-law, while the rest of them turned around and went back to the boat.

"And then what happened?" I said. "Did they get stung?"

"They made it to the island, we picked them up, they were fine!" she said.

We laughed.

We had been standing in the parking lot for a while by then, neither of us making the first move to leave. I wondered aloud what her mother had been thinking at that moment that they'd all turned and gone back to the boat—watching her children and their spouses in retreat. Her mother-in-law, too—what had she been thinking? Fernanda said she wondered about that as well, and that later that night, when they were all sitting together in the hot tub outside the hotel, she asked them. Fernanda's own guess was that, after years of caring for others—their useless husbands, their squabbling children—it felt nice for them to escape for a minute, that facing the stingrays, dangerous as they could be, was better than having to return to all that drama in the boat.

But her mother-in-law said she hadn't thought much of anything at all. "Only—I'd gone this far already, and maybe it was dangerous, but it was also really beautiful. I didn't want you all to get hurt, so I was glad you turned around. But I wasn't afraid for myself. I've had many, many chances to die before—all that cancer—and I'll have many, many chances to die again. I didn't know when I'd get to travel here again, maybe never, and it'd be a shame to stop when I had gone this far."

"That's it, then?" I said.

"That's it, that's all she said about it."

"What about your mother?"

"She said that once she saw my mother-in-law going ahead, she was inspired and thought she could do it, too—and how unexpected and beautiful an experience it had been, how blessed, how lucky it felt to be in God's light."

Puppet Master
Made the Puppets

MEE SCRAPES COCONUT oil from its tub. It melts in her palms like butter. She pretends to eat her hands: "Num, num, num—toast." I sit in Mee's lap. She puts her hands on my head and rubs. I close my eyes. I meow.

"No being cats tonight, okay?"

"Mrow!"

"Okay, okay—mrow, and good night." She goes.

Then it's Dee's slippers thumping down the hall and into the room.

"Good night, little bee."

"Mrow."

At night, I can't sleep. A car comes down the street and sends a square of light across the carpet. Dee shouts at Mee. I'm itchy; I scratch myself.

The morning hurts. Blood on my arms and legs. Brown cream under my fingernails—blood and skin. I use my fingernail to scrape the brown from the other nails. I make a little ball with it.

Hide it in the bathroom drawer behind the safety pins. The next day I make the ball bigger. I roll and roll to make it round. A pearl of blood and skin.

I PRETEND to dive for pearls. I pretend I'm on a boat. I sit in the laundry basket in the backyard, while Mee hangs up the sheets to dry. She doesn't want them to drag in the grass, or Dee will shout, and she will have to wash them again. She hangs them in the shape of a hammock.

AT MY grandparents' house, we eat bannock. I say, "More bannock!" Dee tells Mee, "Get her more!" Mee says, "She'll be sick," and I say, "Then I don't want more." Dee suddenly stands and gets close to Mee, and Mee ducks and puts her arm up over her head. Nothing happens. Dee laughs. Mee goes for the bannock. The bannock is on a paper plate and cut in four pieces. I say I don't want it. Dee says, "It's your favorite." I say, "I'm full."

Once my grandparents took us to see dancing dolls. Flinging arms, flinging legs. "Oh-ee-oh-ee-oh-ee-oh!" People were laughing, even the dolls were laughing, but we weren't laughing. I said, "How do those dolls sing?" Dee said, "They're puppets." I said, "How do the puppets sing?" Nobody said anything. Then Mee said, "There's a puppet master hiding back there to make them sing and dance. Puppet master made the puppets." I said, "Puppet master makes them laugh?"

Mee doesn't like my grandparents, her in-laws; they think we're rich, they fish for money. Mee says, "Easy for people to think others have good lives." Dee says, "But we do have it good!" Mee and

Dee are opposites. Mee never smiles; Dee smiles all the time. Mee is quiet; Dee is loud. Mee works; Dee stays home. When Mee goes to work, we play Cats. We rub our heads on the couch: "Mrow, mrow!" Dee says, "Okay—you want a cat?" I want a cat. But Mee doesn't want a cat. Dee claps his hands and says, "We'll surprise her! Come on—let's go—"

THE SINGER on the radio sings, Let's go! He sings about going crazy, going nuts, a purple banana in a truck.

DEE PEELS a banana, and slices fall out—already cut. He gives me a slice. He claps his hands and says, "Magic!" Our cat is hiding under the table. He's afraid of us. Dee laughs: "Wait till Mee sees!" And: "What should we name him?"

I HAVE a secret with Magic. In the bathroom I show Magic my ball. He says, "Mrow?" Mee hates the cat. Mee says I misbehaved. I tell her: "But Dee took me!" Mee tells me to tell Dee to take Magic back to where he came from. Dee says if we take Magic there, they will kill him. They will wait four days to see if someone comes for him, then they will kill him. My ball is getting bigger and bigger. It will be an egg, an onion, a pumpkin, a beach ball, a snowman's top, a snowman's middle, a snowman's bottom. Wait till my ball is big enough. You wait, Magic. Then I will bring puppet master to life.

*   *   *

I SEE her at night. She curls on the bottom of the bed at my feet next to Magic. Puppet master lives in the night and wants to come to the day. She makes me scratch. She says, Only you can bring me into the day—until you bring me I won't leave you alone in the night. Puppet master wants blood and skin; she wants me to scratch and give her my ball of blood and skin. In the day, she will make us all sing and dance and laugh. Arms around each other's shoulders, legs flinging: Ooh-ee-ooh-ee-ooh-ee! In the night, puppet master says, "In the day, you must sing, 'Ooh-ee-ooh-ee-ooh-ee!' Then I will know you love me, and I will come alive."

IN THE morning, I am bleeding all over. The brown cream pushes out from my fingernails. In the bathroom I sit on the floor and sing, "Ooh-ee-ooh-ee-ooh-ee!" I come out of the bathroom and sing, "Ooh-ee-ooh-ee-ooh-ee!" Dee brings me medicine. Jars and jars. Mee says, "I'm getting a second opinion."

At the clinic, the nurses say, "Hi, ladies!" Mee mumbles. She doesn't want Dee to know we're here. Doctor says to open my mouth. Doctor puts his cold stethoscope on my chest. Doctor holds my elbows in his palms and looks at my arms and says, "And now what do we have here?" Mee says, "It's getting worse—see?" The door opens, and Dee comes in. I go to him: "Dee-ee-ee-ee!" Dee looks at Mee and says, "Thought we decided against this—no offense, Doc." Doctor says to Dee, "Oh, none taken." Mee says, "But I think she's allergic to the cat! Couldn't she be?" Doctor says, "Oh, a cat!" I cry, "It's not his fault, poor Magic!" And I cry. Doctor laughs. "So we're committed to the cat, I see." Dee rubs his head and says, "This little girl has been begging for years—what can I do, Doc?"

*   *   *

IN THE mornings, when I watch the cartoons with Dee, the bunny says Doc. The bunny says, Promenade across the floor. Sashay right on out the door. Out the door and into the glade and everybody promenade. Step right up you're doing fine. I'll pull your beard you'll pull mine. Yank it again like you did before. Break it up with a tug of war. Now into the brook and fish for the trout. Dive right in and splash about. Trout! Trout! Pretty little trout! One more splash and come right out. Shake like a hound dog. Shake again. Wallow around in the old pig-pen. Wallow some more. Y'all know how. Roll around like an old fat sow. Allemande left with your left hand. Follow through with a right-left grand. Now leave your partner, the dirty old thing. Follow through with an elbow swing. Grab a fence post. Hold it tight. Whomp your partner with all your might. Hit him in the shin. Hit him in the head. Hit him again. The critter ain't dead. Whomp him low and whomp him high. Stick your finger in his eye. Pretty little rhythm. Pretty little sound. Bang your heads against the ground. Promenade all around the room. Promenade like a bride and groom. Open up the door and step right in. Close the door and into a spin. Whirl! Whirl! Twist and twirl! Jump all around like a flying squirrel. Now don't you cuss and don't you swear. Just come right out and form a square. Now right hand over and left hand under. Both join hands and run like thunder—

MEE GETS up. Dee sits down. I sit down. Mee sits down. Now we're sitting very still. Mee is mad, because I cried about Magic and made her look bad. Dee is mad, because Mee blamed Magic and made Dee look bad. I am mad, because, Puppet Master, you said you would come soon.

I SCRATCH. I scratch. In the morning, Dee is gone. Only me and Mee and Magic are left. Mee says, "Don't you want to stop scratching? Then we need to take the cat back. When he comes home, you tell him, 'Dee, I want to take the cat back.'" I can't tell Mee that Magic isn't making me scratch—that it's you, Puppet Master. I tell her: "But they'll kill him!" Mee says, "My baby, don't cry," and she cries, too. Magic comes around the corner and pushes me with his head. He pushes Mee with his head. Mee looks at Magic and takes him to her chest and hugs him. Magic pushes his head on her chest, on her arms.

Later, Mee cleans the house. She pulls the cat hairs from the couch cushions. She scratches with her thumbnail at the dried onion bits stuck to the floor. "We'll just have to keep it really clean," she says. She goes into the bathroom. She opens the drawer. She sees my ball and covers her mouth like she will throw up. I don't know if she understands what it is. I want to tell her, but I don't. I know something terrible is about to happen. Mee wraps the ball in a wad of toilet tissue and drops it in the toilet and flushes. I stay in the bathroom and look into the toilet. Where does it all go? Outside the bathroom, Mee is walking through the house with an incense stick. The smoke curls, then disappears. I find her and ask, "Mee—where does the toilet water go?"

Mee says, "To the ocean, I guess."

*   *   *

IN MY favorite book, a pet-seller visits an old woman. She is nice—she takes a canary, a beaver, a woodpecker, a turtle. "But no elephants!" she—Mee—says. The house is cold in winter. The old woman and the animals are afraid of the winter. The elephant is afraid, too. He stands outside the window. One night the old woman dances with her pets to stay warm, and the elephant stands outside in the cold with snow piling on his head, like a mountain. They can hear him crying. So she lets him in. The other animals dance with him. But in the winter, he eats all the food and crashes through the floor, and the old woman is afraid again. When the elephant stands, he lifts the house from the ground and starts to walk. He walks and walks and walks and walks. Sometimes I cry at that part. Mee says, "Shush, the happy part is coming." When the elephant stops, they have arrived on a beach. There is a sign hanging between the palm trees: WEL-COME, ELEPHANTS. The animals relax. The elephant reads a book on a lawn chair, wearing swimming trunks and sunglasses. Mee says, "Told you, sweetie, everyone is happy in the end."

The Eighteen Girls

THE FIRST GIRL'S mother put her in a towering chair. Her sister sat next to her, in a normal chair. "Thumbu, Thumbu," said the first girl's sister—her nickname for the first girl, who she had thought would be a brother. Wherever her sister went, the girl's eyes roved: fridge, counter, trash can. The girl was suddenly afraid she would fall from her chair; she cried out; her sister ran over and put her finger in the first girl's mouth; the first girl sucked on it and slept.

THE SECOND girl watched her father and sister toss a tennis ball in the yard under the crabapple tree. Their elderly white neighbors were barbecuing next door. The second girl's father waved at them. The second girl's sister told her that they were roasting hot dogs. The second girl marveled at the transformation: that a dog could turn from that to this, imagine.

*　　*　　*

WHEN HER sister started kindergarten, the third girl went to the day care next door to her school. During nap time, the teacher left the room, and the third girl walked out to the playground by herself and climbed to the top of the monkey bars to see if she could see her sister from there. She couldn't. She leapt down, fractured her arm, didn't go to day care anymore.

THE FOURTH girl had a clown doll with a round, red, hard nose who told her he was Ronald McDonald's son. The girl pushed her doll in a stroller from one end of the long hall of the floor of their apartment building to the other end, then back, while waiting for her sister to come home from school. Sometimes she and her doll went into their apartment to visit her mother. There, her mother complained about her father and taught the fourth girl to read. Her doll sat beside her. Sometimes she loved him, sometimes she hated him. If you twisted his nose, a song emanated from his insides. He was made of cloth and filled with fuzzy stuffing. She bit at a seam and began pulling out the stuffing. Her sister said that if she kept removing it, only a pile of cloth and fuzz would be left. "Don't be a killer, Thumbu," her sister said. One afternoon, the fourth girl hid under the stairwell and pulled out all the stuffing. She was left with a cloud of fuzz next to her leg, her doll flattened on her lap. Only his nose was the same. She twisted it. The song played. She began to wonder if she was having a nightmare.

ON THE linoleum floor of the kindergarten classroom, near the cubbyholes where the fifth girl was told to leave her backpack, there was a small brown bit stuck to the floor. It had to be a booger. It was the first day of school. She sat at a round table with the other kindergarteners and kept turning to see if it was still there, but it was too small and far; she couldn't tell. School was in Spanish. Necesito ir al baño, she learned. At recess, she nudged the bit with her shoe. She had a plan to push it underneath the cubbies. But it wouldn't move. On the second day of school, she dreaded returning, but her mother made her. The bit was still there. She wondered who it had come from. She asked her sister whether a booger could be thought of as part of a person's body, like their blood or guts or arm; if a booger came out of a person's body and ended up on the floor, did it mean someone had lost a part of themselves? Her sister said she wasn't sure.

One morning, she stood in front of her cubbyhole, her back to the bit, and commanded it to disappear, ¡vete! She turned around, and the bit was still there. "What are you staring at?" a boy named J. T. McDonald said. She didn't dare answer. "Do you know English?" he said. J. T. McDonald told everyone she didn't speak English, and her sister told her mother, and her mother got mad.

"You're the most intelligent child in the class, and they all think you're stupid!" she said.

"Someone's booger is stuck to the floor," she said.

THE SIXTH girl and her sister rode their bicycles to the trail alongside the creek. "Let's ride through it," the sixth girl said.

"That's nuts," her sister said, and then, maybe noticing the mischief in her eyes: "I swear, don't *do* it."

"I'm doing it!" said the sixth girl, and she biked right in. Her sister followed. The sixth girl was thrown over her handlebars and landed in the water. Her sister collided with the sixth girl's downed bike and was flung to the side. They climbed out of the water and watched the creek churning around their bikes. Her sister had a gash on her shin; she was bleeding. They pulled out the bikes, wet and muddied and dented, and walked them home. "I'm sorry," she told her sister. "I'm extremely sorry." Her sister was silent. Her blood was reddening the cuff of her sock.

When they got home, their mother bandaged her sister, then sat them both on the couch and knelt before them with a wearied expression. "What happened?" she said.

"Our bikes went into the creek," her sister said, with her chin in the air.

"Whose idea was it?"

The sixth girl thought her sister would implicate her. "Hers!" she cried preemptively, pointing, as her sister said, "No one's; we fell in."

THE MOTHER of the seventh girl said she was tired of doing everything for everyone else. She signed up for a class in painting ceramics. Once a week her mother disappeared, and her father had to cook dinner. He made delicious shrimp curry—his specialty, he said. But there was a difference between mothers and fathers, her mother said. Fathers hardly ever made dinner, so that when they did, they felt good about it and made the food delicious. Mothers had to do it all the time, on top of shopping, cleaning, taking care of the children. The seventh girl willed her mother to be quiet. Then, as if her mother had heard, she did become quiet.

Her mother brought home a unicorn figurine that she had painted bronze. The unicorn stood with its hind legs on a circular platform, raising its front legs in the air. The girl had never been

prouder of her mother. The unicorn stood on the coffee table. One afternoon, the seventh girl felt tempted to test its strength. She took it in her fist and tapped it, by its spiral horn, on the coffee table. When nothing happened, she tapped harder. This time the horn broke off, leaving only a tiny white circle exposed on its head. Her mother was in the kitchen. Quietly, she took up the unicorn and its horn and went to her sister's room. Her sister gasped and said, "Tráeme el Krazy Glue, ¡ahora mismo!"

The seventh girl went on an expedition to the kitchen. Her mother was standing right there over the stove. The seventh girl opened the drawer and removed the little dented tube of glue and left the kitchen. "Get in here!" her sister hissed from her bedroom. She got in there. Her sister squirted the tiniest drop of glue onto the unicorn's white spot and reattached the horn and sat there for five full minutes, her fingers trembling, holding the horn in place. "Estúpida," she murmured. They returned the unicorn to its spot, and, for a long time, no one learned of the seventh girl's sin.

THE MOTHER of the eighth girl decided to leave the eighth girl's father. The eighth girl's father sat sheepishly on the couch with his hands clasped in his lap. The eighth girl disdained him. It didn't seem difficult to keep a wife. Her mother said each of them could stay with her or with him: their choice. The eighth girl's sister locked herself in the bathroom. The eighth girl whispered to her sister through the door: "Who are you going to choose?"

"I'm still deciding," said her sister. The eighth girl had decided on their mother, but she had a feeling her sister would choose their father.

She waited and waited. Then, through the door, her sister whispered, "You still there?"

"I'm here."

"I thought of a plan to change her mind."

The eighth girl wanted to know the plan, but her sister wouldn't tell her. "Just wait," she said.

"Where?"

"It doesn't matter."

The eighth girl got an Archie comic from her bedroom and sat in the hall outside the bathroom, reading it. "Do you want an Archie?" she whispered to her sister after a while.

"Okay," her sister said.

The eighth girl got another one and slid it under the door. A long time passed while they read. Every so often, the eighth girl's sister requested another Archie. Then their dad came to the hall and said in a tired, irritable voice, "Girls, it's bedtime."

The eighth girl's sister said, from inside, "Where's Mom?"

"Sleeping."

"The eighth girl's sister opened the door and regarded the eighth girl in triumph.

"Well? What's the plan?" the eighth girl said.

"That was it," her sister said.

AFTER SCHOOL, her sister made pasta, and they read magazines together. If you wanted to make a boy fall in love with you, her sister explained, you should mirror his behavior. When he lifts his drink, you should lift yours at the same time. This will make him feel, on a subconscious level, like you are soul mates. They looked up *subconscious*. The mental activities just below the threshold of consciousness. *Consciousness*: the quality or state of being aware,

especially of something within oneself. They sat on her sister's bed and ate pasta and practiced. Her sister lifted her Dr Pepper, and the ninth girl lifted her milk. Her sister shoved her finger in her nose, and the ninth said, "Be serious!"

"It's a load of crap!" her sister said, laughing. "Did you really believe it?"

She said no, but kept watching to see if her sister believed they were soul mates.

"Subconscious," her sister said.

"Subconscious," she said.

THE TENTH girl had a disgusting face. Her sister said to think of the most beautiful girl she had ever met, then pretend to be that girl, and after a while, she wouldn't have to pretend anymore. She would be transformed. There was nothing wrong with transforming yourself. Life itself, she said, transforms us. In each moment of life, you're slightly different from the person you were a moment earlier.

THE ELEVENTH girl and her sister merged into one person. This person was a sixteen-year-old girl named Lauren. Lauren had short hair dyed red and wore a lip ring. She dressed in cut-off T-shirts that bared her pierced belly button. Her skin was poreless. She was a raver and a recovering cocaine addict. Lauren went into chat rooms for pedophiles. She had cybersex with them, and then tried to persuade them to meet in person.

One of them said he would: a forty-three-year-old man named Eugene. They set a date at the movie theater. Her sister didn't have short red hair or piercings, but she was fourteen—close enough to sixteen. They stood in the vestibule of the theater and watched people enter. Men came in, but none were alone. The movie was going to start soon.

Then a small boy, maybe twelve, sidled over and said to her sister, "Is your name Lauren?"

"Who told you to ask me that?" she said.

"Is it?"

"It is."

"I thought you'd be white."

Eugene had olive skin and black hair; he might have been Mexican. He wore an Alanis Morissette T-shirt. The three of them watched *Batman Forever*. Afterward, Eugene told the eleventh girl's sister he wanted to kiss her. She said he couldn't. He said she should at least let him touch her. He had come all the way there. Fine, she said. You can touch my stomach, but only if my sister comes with us. They went behind the theater, and her sister rolled up her T-shirt a little. Eugene put his finger in her belly button.

"Hey!" her sister said, twisting away.

"You said it would be pierced," Eugene said, and he turned and left.

"You said you were forty-three!" the eleventh girl called out after him.

HER SISTER got cancer. The twelfth girl didn't want to visit her sister at the hospital. Instead, she organized a cancer fundraiser at her middle school, where she gave a speech about her sister, bedridden and only a sophomore. Everyone admired the speech, admired her. She had learned how to will herself into being someone else. She wanted to avoid the hospital without looking bad, and what better excuse than a cancer fundraiser?

She bought a piece of poster board and taped it to the wall at school and made an announcement that everyone should write messages to her sister on it. "Hope there are some cute boys at the hospital!" she wrote, hoping that would make her sound cool to the other kids who wrote on the poster. People came up to her in the middle of the hall and hugged her. By the end of the week, the poster board was filled with messages of love and support, pictures, long notes folded into small shapes and taped on, so that when she pulled down the poster, she had to hold it faceup to keep everything from falling off. She took it to the hospital, where her sister muted *Seinfeld* and said, "It's about time you showed up." The twelfth girl said, "Ta-da! Here's what I've been doing all this time!" Her sister peered at the poster for a while, then turned to their parents and shouted, "She told her whole school?"

AMBER-COLORED BOTTLES were arranged on the thirteenth girl's sister's bedside table. The table resembled the religious altars their parents' religious friends set up for their gods, only instead of little brass bowls of colored powders, here was Percocet, Dilaudid, Ativan, and a framed photograph of the sisters as children. The thirteenth girl looked at that picture and felt as if those girls were strangers.

HER PARENTS gave her a hundred-dollar bill. At school under the beige-domed cafeteria, known as the Mushroom, the fourteenth girl hovered near the stoners' table and hoped someone would approach her. What was a person supposed to do: walk up and request drugs from one of them, as you did with the Business Club kids who sold baked goods from behind a booth?

One of the stoners, Big Joe, wore a gas mask and camos to school, and people were afraid of him because of that and his size. It was around the time of the Columbine killings. But she and Big Joe had played policemen together in *The Pirates of Penzance*, and they were friends. Her friends were mostly girls, but in *Penzance*, she had worn a stick-on mustache, and it had emboldened her to befriend the boys. She approached Big Joe, telling herself to pretend to be someone who knew how to buy drugs. "When the foeman bears his steel," Big Joe sang out to her, saluting. "Tarantara! Tarantara!" she replied. But suddenly she lost her nerve.

At home, her father said, "Did you bring it?" She lied: "They didn't have any left. They ran out." She could hear her sister in the background, her voice muffled because of her mouth sores: "That's ridiculous. They don't run out." Her sister was in a lot of pain. She couldn't eat, she could drink only through a straw. Her muscles ached. She couldn't go a half hour without throwing up. Her hair had fallen out. She had lost twenty pounds. Even her face had changed. If she lived—and maybe she wouldn't—she would likely be infertile.

Her father held out his hand, and she returned the hundred-dollar bill. Her father drove to Capitol Hill and returned home with a bulging little plastic bag. He lit a joint with a match. Her sister sucked on it, coughed, smiled.

"Do you feel high?" she asked after a while, leaning in and sniffing her sister's breath.

"No, but I don't hurt as much."

"See?" said their father. "Even Daddy knows how to buy drugs!"

The fourteenth girl ran to the bathroom and slammed the door, humiliated.

*   *   *

HER SISTER became religious. She said she didn't fear death anymore. She had lived well and had found her meaning, which was to love her family and friends and to be loved by them. She claimed God talked to her, in her mind. The fifteenth girl thought her sister was going insane because the cancer was pushing against her brain, which was what—from what she understood—would kill her soon. Her sister took their parents to the Buddhist temple in the International District, where she liked to meditate like Siddhartha under a twisted tree in the temple yard. They also went to Christian churches and to the Hindu temple. She believed it all; to believe in one and not the others, she said, was false belief, because all true belief was one belief. She wrote a poem.

You can say that we're all dying
You can look at it that way
But I don't
Because I'm not
I'm living every day
I'm living every moment
Each one in my own way
I'm living and I'm loving
And all I have to say
Is thank you God
Thank you so much
Thank you for today

The fifteenth girl did not believe in any gods, not a single one of them. The fifteenth girl believed in her sister and herself.

THE SIXTEENTH girl was in the bathroom with her, helping her sister bathe; she didn't have the strength to lift her arms on her own, twist them the way they would need to twist in order to reach the places in need of bathing. "Don't tell Mom and Dad, but I am God," her sister said. She didn't answer. The hospice counselor had said they should go along with her sister's beliefs and not contradict her. It was true, too, that her sister had a god's name, that of Vishnu's eighth incarnation, the blue-skinned god. She said after she died, she would send an eagle to visit the sixteenth girl and help her along in life.

The sixteenth girl said, "I won't tell." Her sister was sitting in the bathtub; she perched on its rim, her clothes on, her feet inside. When she was about to run the washcloth up the base of her sister's head, which was sensitive because of the mass, she stopped and said, "I'm worried it'll hurt." They looked at each other, and at the same time, tears came to their eyes. "That's called a soul connection," her sister said, flushed. "That isn't something people can explain with logic." The sixteenth girl wanted to strip and get into the tub with her sister and hold her until their existences merged, but she said, "I don't feel it."

THE FUNERAL director said they could either have a pine cremation box for free or buy a fancier one made of high-end wood or metal. They said they would bring their own box. The seventeenth girl and her parents bought one at Pier One Imports for four dollars and felt good about having outsmarted the funeral director. It was padded in a purple cloth that had a floral design made of small plastic beads. Purple was—had been—her sister's favorite color. Her sister came out of a refrigerated room on a metal stretcher. She and her parents carried the cold stretcher to a hot room that seemed, because of the furnace in the wall, like a pizzeria. They put their hands on the stretcher and pushed her sister into the oven.

The next day, they returned there, and the funeral director gave them the box. The seventeenth girl sat in her closet with it and shut the door. She opened the box. Inside was a coarse grayish-white sand, with some pebbly bits in it. She put her palm in the sand and made a handprint; her palm came away dusted with it. She licked her hand. The ashes tasted like dust. Eat; this is my body. She pinched a bit more in her fingers and ate it and coughed. She hid the box at the rear of her closet. Across the hall, she could hear her parents tearing up her sister's bedroom searching for the ashes. Her father thought her mother had lost the ashes, and her mother was suspicious that her father had scattered them on his own. Then their voices grew quiet. She expected to become nauseous, but the afternoon passed into evening, and she was not.

FROM TIME to time, notions drifted into the eighteenth girl's mind that she didn't believe at all—religious notions—and she understood that this was the voice of her sister speaking from within her. Here I am; weep not. Truly, truly, I say to you, whoever hears my word and believes him who sent me has eternal life. There was never a time when I, you, or these kings did not exist; nor shall we ever cease to exist in the future.

What Next

MY DAUGHTER AND I have checked into our hotel room, and from here it's all arranged. At seven o'clock, her father will meet her in the hotel lobby and take her out to eat—for an hour and a half, at most. He agreed to this over the phone last month. I also explained to him in that phone call—our first in a decade and a half—about the lies I had been telling Mayuri about her parentage. I begged him not to reveal the truth when they met in person. He laughed, as if we were on good terms, as if we were friends. "Babe, calm down! I'm on it. We're going to have a great time!"

These words have often roared into my mind since that conversation, and each time, they becalm me—ha-ha, no, they becalm me not. They came to me a moment ago, as I watched Mayuri, my tall, fat-cheeked, curly-haired girl, sitting cross-legged on the bed in a sweatshirt and jeans, drumming her fingers on her knee-caps. It's six o'clock, one hour to go. Babe, calm down.

I lift our suitcase onto the bed next to her and open it,

rummaging for something to wear. I hold a lemon-colored sweater in one hand and an oversized floral button-down in the other: "This or this?" I'm thinking of what Charlie would see in each. I want him to see a stranger and feel unsettled.

"You're not the one going out," Mayuri says.

Mayuri turned eighteen three months ago. Almost her whole life I have been telling her lies—one foundational lie at the beginning, that her father was a sperm donor, and then little decorative lies over the years, cupolas, friezes, lintels of untruth. They didn't matter. She considered me her only parent, our relationship a closed loop, our mutual devotion complete. It was only recently that she changed, bringing up the stories I had told as if they were fact and wanting to know more. At the age of sixteen, she mentioned genetic testing. I panicked. I told her that I wouldn't allow it, she was too young, she could decide for herself when she was eighteen.

Then she turned eighteen.

"I'm going to find a restaurant while you're with him—I need to eat, too," I tell her. "I'm craving Thai food." I leave the clothes on the bed and go to the window to see if it's still raining. Water spills down the outside of the window in thick rivulets, and the sky is dull and grayish. I had thought California was supposed to be full of sunshine and pleasantness. But then, I have thought all kinds of wrongheaded thoughts in my life.

"Welcome to California," I say—the gloom of it feels like an omen.

"The flowers," she tells me, softening.

The flowers, then. I put the shirt on, and Mayuri and I take the elevator downstairs. The lobby is old-fashioned, almost grand. A young couple in hiking gear sit sunken in plush armchairs.

There is a bar in the corner and even a piano in the middle of the room.

"Can I play it?" Mayuri says. She was enthralled by the piano the first time we came across someone playing one, in a shopping mall, when she was young. Immediately, she begged me to let her learn. I resisted—the lessons a luxury we couldn't afford—but, over the months that followed, she wore me down. I saved and saved and bought a scratched and faded old upright and three months of classes. At first, she didn't seem to have a feel for it at all; she played tentatively, hunched over the keyboard like a beginning typist. But after some time, the instrument unleashed her. She became obsessed with that piano; and as she grew older, she developed a strange, full-bodied style of playing that gave the impression that the instrument had attached itself to her, like an appendage. She would clamp down with her fingers, head lolling, back arched. It almost frightened me. I hoped it was a phase, but her relationship with the piano only became more intense. At recitals, she gets standing ovations, every time. It reminds me of Charlie, the theatrics of it.

"Not now," I tell her. And then: "Where should we wait for him?" My voice sounds shrill to myself. I wonder if Mayuri notices.

If she does, she doesn't show it. Instead of answering my question, she crosses the lobby and goes for the bar. The bar! I follow her. She plants herself on a barstool; I sit next to her. The bartender, a rangy, mustachioed man with a tattoo of a typewriter on his forearm, notices Mayuri before he notices me. She's too young—he must be thinking—to be sitting at a bar. But he smiles and says to her, "What can I get you?"

"I'll have a glass of white wine, please, the pinot grigio," I tell him. "Nothing for her."

"We have virgin stuff," the bartender says to her. He's young, but he must be at least twenty-one—I don't like the word *virgin* on his tongue.

"Pick one for me?" she says.

"You got it," the bartender says, grinning at Mayuri.

"How old are you?" I ask him.

"Twenty-one," he says, startling.

"This is my daughter, and she only just turned eighteen," I say, as he pours my wine. I know what I sound like, but I cannot help it. Not at a time like this—a time of high stakes.

Mayuri is wearing only minimal makeup—lip gloss, mascara. She doesn't look like trouble. But, when she was seventeen, I caught her sending naked photos of herself to older men. She took them herself: In one, she's on her bed covering her breasts with one arm, while the other extends out, as if to embrace the viewer. She's wearing her hair in two braids and chewing on half of her lower lip. Even after I grounded her and lectured her and deleted the evidence, the memory of the pictures filled me with terror. I realized I had become one of those mothers who other mothers pity—a mother who has failed to protect her child.

"Happy birthday to her, then," the bartender says, and he wields Mayuri's drink in the air—lemon, hibiscus, tonic water—as if to make a toast. He does this with an amused expression. I perceive danger in it. Under the typewriter tattoo is the word WRITER. These men. I cannot understand if he is making fun of me, flirting with Mayuri, or both. He lowers his arm and pretends he's about to take a gulp of the drink. "Hey!" Mayuri shouts, standing and swiping her hand at his. "Give it!" Several men turn to stare. "Come on!" she cries.

He laughs and gives her the glass.

"Are you a writer?" she asks him.

"I am."

"My dad is one, too," she tells him.

MAYURI HAS far more ease with men than I ever did. Growing up in India at her age, I was fixated only on school. I had been gifted at math, had known my multiplication tables by the age of six, and not only my parents but our whole small town was convinced that if any girl could leave there and go abroad, just as upper-caste girls from bigger cities were doing—which was the mark, at the time, of having succeeded—it was me. I disdained the girls who developed crushes on the local hooligans who would bike past and yank their dupattas. I dreamed of being a doctor. But my parents weren't rich—my father was a teacher in our small town—and, when it came time to decide how to spend their limited savings, they took the conservative route. After I finished my undergraduate studies, instead of sending me on to medical college, they found me a husband who worked as a doctor in the U.S.; the plan was for me to get married and apply to medical school there.

That husband was a perfectly fine person. His patients liked him. He was quiet and careful and didn't require too much of me. At night, he would stand in front of the bathroom mirror in his undershirt, brushing his teeth in small, controlled circles, his posture erect, and then get into bed and squeeze my shoulder and sleep. I kept waiting for a chance to bring up medical school, but it seemed presumptuous to do it before we'd established a proper marital rapport; I worried he'd believe—rightly—that I'd had an ulterior motive in marrying him. So I tried to love him first.

We lived in a quiet town in North Dakota. A river ran through it. A river ran through my hometown, too, but there the similarities stopped. In this town, people stayed indoors, their curtains drawn. While my husband was at his clinic, I would wander the quiet streets, feeling anxious. I told myself I was anxious because I missed my husband. I thought, I must love him. I was quiet in that period, too; the quiet town and my quiet husband had turned me quiet. I was supposed to spend a year settling in, and then apply to graduate school. Then my husband was diagnosed with cancer, and for three years, I cared for him. I became more anxious—that he would die—and thought, All right, now it's certain that I love him. But caring for him, by myself, was extremely difficult. When he died, I grieved, at first, but soon felt relief.

My mother, though, was beside herself. When a husband dies, the wife is seen to have brought bad fortune onto his head—she's seen as a bringer of death. How would they find another man—she worried—for this death-bringing daughter of theirs? How enormous must the dowry be to compensate for the death-bringing? They'd drained their savings to get me married the first time. They'd assumed that, as a doctor, my husband would be well-off, but in fact he'd left me with a lot of debt—medical bills, the house to pay off. My mother wanted me to come home and stay with them until we could figure out what to do next, but I couldn't stand the thought. It was partly that I felt responsible for the situation and didn't want to burden them, and partly that I blamed them for having gotten me into the situation in the first place. Their reasoning, in marrying me off instead of sending me to finish my studies, was that we had been solving two problems at once: that of my marriage and that of my studies. Instead, we'd solved neither. I said to my mother that they shouldn't find someone, that I would do it myself.

But I was in my mid-twenties by then, and I had never learned how to meet a man. To support myself, I found a secretarial job at the office of another Indian doctor, an acquaintance of my husband's. In the evenings, after the doctor left, I would read all the notes he had made about his patients and the prescriptions he had written and imagine that they had been written in my hand. The cases were interesting. Sometimes people chopped off their fingers with farm equipment, and the doctor would send them to Bismarck with the finger in a cup of ice. I imagined inheriting the practice after his retirement. I would learn surgery myself. I'd seen the physician's accounts; I imagined you could charge a lot for reattaching a finger. I would build a mansion for myself, another for my parents, another for each auntie and uncle back home who had believed I would make the town proud, another for each former classmate and the dupatta-pulling beau she had married. Mansions would rise up all around our town's stout plaster statue of Dr. Ambedkar, and it would be said all through the district that our collective belief in me had not been for naught.

The doctor had no inkling of my ambition. His wife tried to set me up with Indian bachelors. There were only a handful of them in the entire state, identified through word of mouth; they had to be lured to our town for an evening and they always arrived looking ragged and irritable. I hated how those men looked at me, as if they were doing me a favor. They would sit across the table at the other doctor's home, talking in my direction while mostly trying to impress the other doctor's wife, so that she would introduce them to other, better prospects in the future. They all looked the same, too, the men: short, round-bellied, with pleased-with-themselves expressions. I tell this as if I rejected them for it, but the truth is that the doctor's wife used up all her contacts and ran out of bachelors. None of them wanted me. She was about to start looking in the neighboring states, South Dakota and Montana and Minnesota, but I told her, Stop, that's enough.

And then he appeared, like a boon from the gods. Charlie. He was a patient. He had nice teeth. A strong, hard face; olive skin; a playful, dimpled smile that did not seem condescending. He asked if I was Indian, and I said yes. He said he knew it. But he had mistaken me for the other kind of Indian, more common in North Dakota. He said he had some of that kind of Indian—Sioux, Dakota—in his blood. He asked me on a date right there in the doctor's office. He was a businessman; he owned a shop, inherited from his father, that sold farm equipment. I couldn't believe my good fortune. It was his handsomeness that had drawn me in at first, but what made me accept the date was the thought of all my debt. He could help me pay it off. He could send me to medical school. I wasn't thinking of myself. I was thinking of my mother, whom I had let down without meaning to. I had spoken to her only twice since I told her I would find my own husband, though she wrote to me, asking me to call. I had never been lonelier in my life.

In my hometown, there had been an expression: "You should live in a place with someone who can heal, someone who can lend you money, someone who can take care of your soul, and an ever-flowing source of water." It was an old expression, but people still used it, because the town hadn't ever changed. In my restless adolescence, the expression had reminded me of how limited everyone else's desires were compared to my grander ones. But I thought of it differently after my husband died. I walked along the river and thought of how this town, despite its location in the country of my dreams, was worse off than my hometown, by the standard of our expression: No doctor here would erase my late husband's medical bills; no moneylender would be shamed into forgiving the interest; no priest would speak the language of my soul. I kept thinking I would call my parents when I had a husband in hand. Now a prospective one had appeared. I wanted Charlie to pick me up, right there, and carry me over the threshold of his home; I was committed in that moment. Only later did I realize he went around asking women on dates wherever he went. He went on dates all the time.

We had dinner—on our particular date—at the Koko House. We sat on cushions on the floor, on either side of a low candlelit table, and he taught me to use chopsticks. He told me that he was still looking for the right person and wasn't going to settle down with the wrong one just to satisfy bourgeois conventions. That was his phrase, *bourgeois conventions*, and I made a note to myself to remember it. He said he was a writer—a poet—and this thrilled me. I used to love reading—Jane Austen, Charles Dickens. Charlie said he wasn't close with his parents, though they lived in town. They were people, he said, of limited imagination. That, too, was his phrase, *limited imagination*. He was afraid of turning into them. He had seen it happen before—first, his grandfather turning into his great-grandfather, then his father turning into his grandfather. It made him feel desperate, he said, the thought of doing the same. He couldn't bear to inherit the store.

To me it had always seemed magical—the idea that each of us is one link in an unbroken chain. My mother had given birth to me at the age of fourteen, and after that, she had refused to have any more children. It had been the boldest move of her life. She herself had been the oldest of four children and the only girl. She had wanted to go to college, but her father wouldn't let her. He said her mother needed help raising her brothers. She didn't want the same to happen to me; she wanted me to have a good life; it was she who planted my ambition in me. I, too, belonged to a familial chain. In my case, the chain had been so much more tenuous than

I'd understood it to be. Sometimes, I felt my parents had failed me; sometimes, I felt I had failed them. But now—listening to Charlie— I thought maybe the failure had been in our insistence on a chain in the first place. Our belief that this mutual responsibility—them to me, and me to them, trapping us in a cycle of resentment and shame—should be inevitable.

"Then don't," I said. "Sell the store! Write your poems!"

Soon after that date, he put the shop up for sale and began devoting himself to his writing. He stopped by the clinic to tell me. He called it a gesture of protest against the Reaganite ideals that our country hadn't yet shaken. *Reaganite ideals.* He sounded like a professor, all those brilliant phrases and words tossed into conversations, *indoctrination, equal opportunity, unalloyed.* His conviction impressed me—his belief in an independent selfhood, unbound to anyone else's. The thought came to me that my aspiration of being a doctor hadn't originally been mine at all; it had belonged first to my mother, who, even before I could articulate my own desires, started going around telling everyone in town that I would be a doctor and live abroad. I thought of what it had been like to care for my dying husband—it had oppressed me, it had felt unnatural, I didn't have a doctor's temperament at all.

I started spending more time with Charlie. He was a fan of the writers Raymond Carver and Richard Brautigan. Brautigan's mother, he told me one night at the Koko House, used to sift rat droppings from their flour rather than throw out the beshitted flour—*beshitted,* another one of those words of his. I told him that in my hometown, all the mothers did this; one needn't be poor to sift droppings from flour. He laughed, and I felt it—his laugh—as a great triumph. That night, he took me home to his house, which had stacks of books piled on the floor. He picked them up one at a time and read lines to me. Then he said, "Come here, you're so damned shy," and he unbuttoned my blouse and kissed me, full-mouthedly, on my collarbone.

THE BARTENDER asks what Mayuri's name is, and she tells him. She adds, "I'm thinking about changing it."

"Changing it!" I cry out.

She gets off her stool and stands next to it, her hands on her hips.

"Ma, look at me," she says. "Look me in the eye and tell me I still look like a Mayuri."

Mayuri hardly ever calls me Ma anymore, so when she does, I get a deep rush of feeling for her. She still stands like a little girl—stomach out, feet splayed—but in the past few years, she has grown tall and strong-boned. She has a gypsy blade of a nose, and eyelids crowded with lashes. Her black hair is as coarse and unruly as a horse's mane. I think of how I must look to her—this matronly dumpling, thin hair getting grayer every day, eyeglasses too large for her face, complexion leather-worn, this aging ma. Mayuri has never resembled me. She is a beaut, to use another one of Charlie's words. I will not lie. She resembles him.

"Tell me I look like a Mayuri," she says, pushing her face out at me.

"She doesn't," says the bartender. "She's right."

It's the color of her skin—people assume she is white. It's her self-confidence in a land in which I have never stopped feeling like a stranger. I look my daughter in the eye, my jaw tight, and I tell her, "You look just like a Mayuri to me, baby-love." I am her mother. The right to name her belongs to me.

IT'S NOT as if there weren't warning signs.

The first was that Charlie was an equal-opportunity charmer, the kind of man who would be chatting up the waitress as I showed up to meet him. The second warning sign was that he lied. Once, he gave me a story he said he had written. It was short, only a couple of pages. It was about a man whose wife and children have left him. He is at home feeling lonesome, when another man comes to his home. That second man has hooks where his hands should be. He wants to sell the first man a photograph he has taken of the first man's house. The second man says that he had children, too, once; his children are the cause of his hook-handedness. The first man says he wants the second man to take pictures of him outside of his house. They go outside. The photographer takes more pictures. When I finished reading it, he asked what I thought.

I said I liked it, but I had a lot of questions. He'd need to resolve these questions, I thought, before anyone published it. What about the first man's wife and children? A man's wife doesn't just leave for no reason. Where had she gone, taking their children along, and what for? How, most importantly, had the second man's children turned his hands into hooks?

Charlie became agitated. He admitted then that he had misled me: He had not written the story after all, Raymond Carver had; it was considered a classic. He had shown it to me to see if I respected him. But I didn't respect him, he said, and now he knew it. We were in his house. Winter had arrived, and he kept his house cold. It turned my fingertips white. He said I was too sensitive, that I needed to learn to adapt. I kept waiting for my fingertips to stop turning white, but they didn't. I touched Charlie's shoulder with my numb fingertips and told him I respected him. I told him I wanted to get married. He said he couldn't marry someone with whom he hadn't shared a roof.

Not long after that, I moved in with Charlie. I redoubled my efforts at proving myself, but the more I tried, the more distant he seemed. "What kind of people keep saying, 'I love you, I love you, I love you,' over and over?" he said. "The kind of people who aren't actually in love and are trying to bullshit themselves into believing they are." I love you, I thought. I love you.

One morning at work, the doctor's wife visited to drop off his lunch, and she pulled me aside. It didn't look good, she said, living with a man to whom I wasn't married. I told her that it would be all right, I would be married soon.

It wasn't long before I got pregnant. The night I told Charlie, he seemed jubilant. He tapped his finger on my belly, *boop*, as if to say hello to her, and I laughed. Marry me, I thought.

Then one night, *boop*, he didn't come home.

IT'S NEARLY seven o'clock. Mayuri stands, rakes both hands through her hair, and looks toward the sliding door at the front of the hotel.

"You're nervous," I say.

"No, I'm not," she snaps.

What I want to tell her is that I will protect her forever. But I can't. Mayuri glances at the bartender, but he doesn't notice. He's leaning on his elbows at the other end of the bar, chatting with a petite redhead closer to his age. I wonder if I'll be able to pinpoint Charlie as he walks in. I see a well-built man in a university T-shirt, but he's walking too fast, not with Charlie's slow, sure lope. Others follow, but they all seem unremarkable. Then one of the unremarkable ones comes in and sees us.

THIS IS what I noticed the first time I held Mayuri.

Her eyes were already open. By the time she reached my arms, twisting like a big fish, she had already seen a bit of the world: the doctor's hands in their wet gloves; the sharp, bisecting lines of a pair of scissors; a flash of the floor, maybe. She wouldn't have found meaning in any of it, I thought, it would have been just shapes to her. The gloves wet from our placental mucus. Scissors meant for cutting. The hard white hospital floor that, to me, was a potential hazard would have been, to her, only a flat plane. When I held my child that morning, I felt relief, exhaustion, wonder, greed, terror—but also something else, a feeling that the borders of my selfhood had opened up and enveloped her. I whispered the name I had chosen, pulled her close to my chest, kissed the top of her head. She was wailing; I marveled at how she wailed, the big noise of it from so little a creature. I nursed her. She stopped wailing. I held her close and murmured some nonsense sounds, the sort of elemental sounds women have sung to our babies since the beginning of motherhood, meaning, we are one, we are one, we are one, we are one.

In those first weeks, I couldn't be away from my daughter without feeling a seizing-up in my chest, a thin, rattling panic. My god—what had I let happen? I had made a mistake with Charlie, but I couldn't work out the math. It was Charlie who had left me to raise our extraordinary daughter on my own; without Charlie, our extraordinary daughter wouldn't exist. It was Charlie who had convinced me to discard all of my long-held beliefs in favor of his; if I hadn't, our daughter wouldn't exist. It was irresolvable. All I could think to do was to flee—to take Mayuri someplace where the mistake wouldn't feel so present. I wanted nothing more than to go home to my mother, who used to console me with buttered bread and a tin cup of warm milk to dip it in. But I couldn't do that to her.

It was the doctor's wife who helped me move to Seattle, for a fresh start. She found me another doctor there who needed an office manager, and paid our bus fare and a month of rent. On our first afternoon, I discovered a small store with Indian spices. I believed it to be a good omen and cooked a feast. I imagined taking Tupperwares to the neighbors' doors and introducing myself. Then, the building supervisor knocked on the door to chastise me for the smells on an unnamed neighbor's behalf, and afterward, I looked upon all of them with suspicion. I tossed out the spices in spite. It occurred to me that I couldn't return to being the person I had once been. I couldn't return to being my mother's daughter. The question of whether my mother's daughter was destined to be a doctor or something else—it was moot. That daughter no longer existed.

But here was Mayuri; here was another chance. She had her own bedroom, but for a long time, she slept in mine, her arms flung around my neck. At nighttime, I invented stories about a mother who wanted a child so much that she went to a magician who could plant a girl-seed inside her.

She was such a spirited child. When she grew older, she would wander the halls of our building, going into whichever neighbor's door happened to be open and plopping herself down on their couches. She had more friends in that building than I did. It was Charlie's charisma that she had inherited. One afternoon when she was about five, she was sitting at the kitchen table after quiet time, eating saltines. I asked her, casually, if she remembered her father. She looked surprised and said no—of course she didn't, she didn't have one.

I froze. I made up a convoluted explanation—another lie— suggesting that people sometimes retain memories of their birth parents in their genetic code even if they've never met them.

"Can I have some peanut butter?" she said.

Maybe it emboldened me—her casual acceptance. When the

time came to explain how babies entered the world, I told her about intrauterine insemination. I said that the donor had been handsome, that I had seen a photo of him, and then I described Charlie, his strong-boned swarthiness, the shine of mischief in his eyes.

And then, a letter arrived. Mayuri was ten. It came when she was at school, addressed to me; I recognized the handwriting, though there was no return address. But when I opened it, I found a letter written to her, not me. "I've been wanting to write to you for a long time," it said, "but I thought I should wait until you could read this letter yourself." He had gotten our address, he wrote, from the doctor's wife. The doctor's wife had told him a little about her—Mayuri—but he wanted to know more. What were some of her hobbies? Did she have any of his qualities—did she consider herself to have an artist's mind? It went on like this, ending with a request that she tell me hello and ask me to let her write back to him sometime. He hoped, he wrote, that they could start to get to know each other. I looked at the envelope again, to see if it had a return address after all, but it didn't. Nor did the letter include one.

I refolded the letter, then put it in a shoebox at the top of my closet. One day when she's old enough—I thought—I'll share this with her. Three months later, another letter arrived. In this one, he wrote that he guessed her mother hadn't let her respond. He understood. But he would keep writing, if that was all right with her. And he did—from then on, a new letter arrived every three or four months. They were progressively more intimate: He wrote that he had moved to California, was working in the restaurant business, had published some short stories. His parents—her grandparents—were alive and well. They were kind people, he wrote. I read all the letters, then hid them in the same box.

Eventually I had told my parents about Mayuri. They had accepted it and asked me to bring her to visit. But I couldn't do it. I couldn't bear thinking of how we would all be seen. Better, I thought, to stay here.

By the time Mayuri was in high school, the letters from Charlie had slowed, but they still arrived, twice or thrice a year. They still came in an envelope with no return address—still addressed to me, not her, which made me feel, on some level, that he was leaving it up to me to decide what to do with them. Increasingly, Charlie's tenebrous presence at the margins of her life seemed menacing to me. Mayuri had grown into a chaotic, distractible teenager. She was as brilliant as ever, but she had no patience for assignments and exams; it wasn't interesting to her, she'd explain, unperturbed, when I'd ask why she hadn't turned in a paper or studied for an exam. By the eleventh grade, she was earning Bs, then Cs and Ds. Every time I brought up college, she said she didn't need to go. Charlie, again, came to mind. His genes—his artist's genes, his chain-breaker's genes—were as much a part of her as mine. Then came the photos.

When she turned eighteen, I bought her the genetic test, as a gift. I thought it unlikely that she'd find him, and at least she'd feel some relief if she could learn more about her heritage, the paternal side of it. Knowing her roots might settle her spirit. I sat with her as she swabbed her mouth, drove with her to the post office to send it off, sat next to her at the kitchen table as she signed into the website to find out the results of the test. She was half-Indian, no surprise. The other half was a mix—Scottish, Mexican, German, Spanish, Italian, Russian, and, yes, Indigenous American. He hadn't lied about that. I was looking at the pie chart when Mayuri gasped, "Ma, look!" She pointed to a message on the left side of the screen: "We've found relatives," it read.

It was a niece who provided his mailing address. I told Mayuri that it was her decision whether to write to him. She let me read the letter. It was brief, cordial. She said she understood that he'd been the sperm donor that her mother used, and she'd be interested in hearing from him if he'd like, but that she didn't expect it. It took all my self-control not to slip my own note into the envelope, explaining the lies and begging him to maintain them.

When a letter came back—with Charlie's name and an address, for the first time, on the top left-hand corner—it had Mayuri's name written on it, not mine. I watched her read it, her mouth widening into a grin. Quickly, she flipped through the pages. "He wrote so much!" she said, with a reverence that I hated to hear. "He wants me to visit!"

HE'S HOLDING an umbrella and wearing jeans and a plain sweatshirt over a paunchy stomach. He gets closer, and, my God, that's him, that ambling grace. He has a full head of hair and a dark beard. Under his beard, his fresh, olive complexion—he still looks young. I wanted to see him and feel superior. Instead, I'm hit with a bolt of something that I had almost forgotten, simultaneous desire and fear. I stand up, skittish; I don't want to scare him off, this time not for my sake but for hers. Mayuri is facing me at the bar, her back to the hotel entrance. She's bent over her phone, finger scrolling—she doesn't see him. He looks at me. His mouth opens a little. He shakes his head. Then he turns and, moving fast this time, walks out.

Mayuri doesn't seem to have noticed. She remains hunched over her phone, sullen-faced. Then, abruptly, she stands and moves to a corner of the bar, where she slouches in an overstuffed armchair.

"What?" she hisses as I approach—not looking at me, the corners of her mouth turned downward as if she's tasted something rancid.

"Give him time," I murmur. "He might be running late."

"He's not—he *texted.*"

"Oh, did he?"

"He said he had a family emergency—he had to leave town."

I try to keep my face calm. "What happened?"

"He didn't say what. He doesn't know when he'll be back. He'll reimburse us for the plane tickets."

"The plane tickets!" My nerves are hot; they overtake me. "Fine, but is he going to reimburse us for my time, and yours?"

"It's fine, I don't care, he's a stranger, he has nothing to do with us. I just thought it would be fun to meet the sperm donor—like, a story I could tell my friends, that's all."

"It's not right—to treat someone like this. You're a child."

"It's an emergency, Ma."

"That's what he claims." There's fire in my voice that I didn't intend.

I wish I could tell her what happens next—whether he'll return, and what next, and what next, and what next. I want nothing more than to narrate for her the story of her life so she can be prepared; I want to warn her about the plot twists, the unreliable characters. What next. What next. What next. And when I'm gone—what then?

"You don't know him," she says, suddenly fierce, as if she's defending him.

How I want to tell the truth. The words are in my throat; I open my mouth to let them escape. "You're right, I don't," I say instead.

Mayuri shakes her head at me, a slight smile on her lips. I don't know what she means by it. Suddenly I'm convinced that she already knows the truth—that she's known it for years, that she found my stash of letters long ago and has been reading them all along. She stands up, leaves the bar, and walks into the lobby. I think for a panicked moment that she's going to go outside. I think she's going to run off to search for him, never to return.

Instead she heads to the piano in the center of the room. She sits on the bench. She bounces a bit, getting comfortable. At the bar, the redhead is talking to a friend who has come to meet her. The bartender leans his elbow on the bar, grips a corkscrew, and watches my daughter.

Mayuri presses her foot on a pedal and leans forward, as if she's listening carefully for some cue. Then she pounces, nearly standing on the pedals, and pounces again, filling the room with a strange, discordant mess of noise—not the sound of a girl playing piano at all, but the sound of a piano coming to life and crunching through the streets on its paws, stepping on pets and children, thrusting itself into traffic, looking to exact revenge on everyone who has laid hands on it. The floor vibrates. My wine ripples in its glass. The bartender widens his eyes at me. A man in an armchair caps his ears with his palms and looks around: Is someone in charge? But there is someone in charge; it's her, it's her, it's my daughter, it's Mayuri. She's raising her hands in the air and slamming them into the piano, and—look at her—she is an astonishment, she is a miracle. For a moment, watching her, I believe she will be fine in this world.

Sibyls

AVA GARDNER WAS going to die. She used one of the *Ency-clopedia Britannica* volumes, from *Shuválov, Peter Andrei-vich* to *subliminal self*, to press her front door in place against the peeling wall. She wouldn't let any of us close the door, and she fastened all the windows in her little apartment so that the wind wouldn't push it shut, either. This was because she was waiting for her husband, she told us. She sat slumped in her armchair facing the door, her blanket pulled to her chin. Every evening, when I knocked on the doorframe to give her dinner, her eyes would flicker open, and she would shout at me to set the plate on the coffee table, pour her a glass of water, and then get out of there, get out, get out. It had to do with the husband: "He won't want to visit with anyone when he gets home, that's for sure." Or else: "He'll be here soon, so I have a lot of cleaning to do, don't I?"

We didn't know which of her husbands she meant; there had been three, a baker, a typewriter repairman, and a nurse. I was eleven years old and had never known a dying person, but I felt they were supposed to act in certain ways, and it bothered me that

Ava didn't fulfill those expectations. When she talked about her husband, she wasn't sentimental. She sounded irritated instead, as if his impending return bugged her. And she never thanked me when I brought her dinner and put a straw in a cup of water. "Go, go, go. He's going to be here any minute."

I looked up Peter Andreivich Shuválov on the internet, but nothing came up. Not a word. If it weren't for that encyclopedia under Ava Gardner's door, it would have been like he hadn't existed at all.

I was getting paid to bring her dinner. Her daughter lived in Minnesota and had hired our neighbors Bonita and Mariam to watch after Ava. It was cheaper for the daughter than putting Ava in a nursing home, my mom explained, and Bonita and Mariam could use the extra cash. Bonita, who lived next door to Ava, worked as a dancer at night, so she took the day shift. Mariam, who lived next to us, a floor down from Ava and Bonita, worked as a security guard during the day, so she took the night shift. For the two hours in between, six o'clock to eight o'clock, Ava was alone. Instead of explaining all this to Ava's daughter and having her pay me, Mariam got paid starting at six o'clock but gave me the first two hours' worth of wages. I brought Ava's dinner up, and if she needed anything else, she rang a bell her daughter had given her. It was easy to hear because her door was open, and ours often was, too, and if we didn't hear at first, she rang the bell until we did.

Ava used to be nice. But several months earlier, her knees had buckled as she stood in front of the building fumbling to get her key into the heavy industrial door. She had dropped onto the cement and broken her hip. She had sat there on the walkway for ten minutes, clenching her teeth, not even calling for help. Because she was proud, my mom said. Too proud. Finally M. Piotrowski, who lived on the first floor, found her and drove her to the emergency room. The hospital put her in a rehabilitation center through the end of the summer, and when she came back, she had changed. She had lost a lot of her hair at that rehab place. Now her marbled forehead sloped all the way to the top of her head. She had turned against us, too. All day long, she sat huddled in her armchair, waiting for her husband and shouting at us.

HUSBANDS. A complicated topic.

Mariam and my mom had met, years ago, in a support group for battered women. But Mariam was still married to her abusive husband, while my mom had divorced hers—my father, a man I didn't remember. Both regretted their decisions. Ever since I had known Mariam, she came over to our place alone, because my mom and Mariam's husband didn't get along. Mariam was big-breasted and fat-limbed, and she sat at the kitchen table and leaned back in her chair like a man. Her voice, too, was loud and strong like a man's. She didn't look like someone you would mess with, but her husband beat her. This was one of the great mysteries of my childhood. Other abused women had this hangdog, sufferers' air about them—my mom was one of them—but not Mariam.

One evening that fall, she and I sat at the table as my mom made dinner. Mariam took out a handkerchief and wiped her forehead. She told us about how it had started to smell like a sewer in Ava's apartment. When Mariam had opened a window that morning to air it out, Ava had hobbled over and looked out just as Bonita was coming home from work, and shouted, "Tramp!" Bonita was wearing a halter top and a miniskirt. Before Mariam could do anything, Ava had cleared her throat and hocked a glob of phlegm down at poor Bonita.

"Did it hit her?" I said.

"Nah, she's fine," Mariam said.

"Man, Ava got so mean," I said. "People say she should have been using her key card like everyone else. Then she'd still be fine. But she insisted on using her keys."

"Remember we'll all get old, too," Mariam said. She wore a big black sweatshirt with an image of a unicorn head made out in silver sequins. Some of the sequins had fallen off, and it gave the unicorn a sad, beat-up look. "Whoever said that to you—those people are going to get old, too, and they'll fall, too, and their neighbors will tell each other, 'Oh, they should have used their key cards.'"

"But it's true, she should have," my mom said.

"I'm telling you, people! She would have fallen, anyway," Mariam scolded. "The key card isn't the problem. The problem is you people are afraid to face your own death. So you tell each other, 'Hey, we're different from her! We use our key cards, so we'll never fall!'"

"It's a lot easier, the key card," my mom muttered.

"I'm sure I'll get demented when I'm old," Mariam said. "I might think I was never married, or I might think Ali's still a baby." Her son Ali had gotten expelled from school the previous year for bringing a gun to school, and now lived in Tacoma with his uncle—his father's brother—and aunt. "I'll run around telling people, 'I have to nurse him, I have to nurse him.' Maybe your mom and me should write you two an instruction manual about how to take care of us. But even then, there's going to have to be a footnote. Right? 'Note that all the lessons in this manual are maybe no good anymore, because we wrote it when we were forty, and now we're eighty-five.' Anyway, Ava doesn't criticize her husbands anymore. I think bad memories die when people stop thinking straight."

"Her husbands were bad?" I said.

"The first and second ones were bad. Third one was okay. He died in the eighties. I think he's the one who's coming for her."

"None of them are coming for her," I said.

"I mean in her head."

"Well, I think it's so sad that she still feels like she has to clean for him all the time. 'He'll be here soon, so I'd better clean!'" my mom said. On the stove, she prodded some meatballs with a spatula. "Dolly, the table?"

"It gives her meaning," Mariam said. "To have something to do."

I took three plates from the dish tray and set them on the table. Paper towels, forks. Water glasses.

"*Meaning*," my mom said. She came over with the strainer and slid some spaghetti onto each plate. Then she brought over the frying pan and spooned a couple of glistening meatballs on top of the spaghetti. "Fancy turkey meatballs," she said. "Okay, Doll, here's what you do. You take ground turkey meat and mix it up with bread crumbs and egg. Then you make big balls and fry them in a frying pan." She was trying, I could tell, to talk about something simple—not about abusive husbands, not about getting old, not about Mariam's lost son. "Mariam's favorite," she said.

Mariam told us about Chinese chicken. You mix up some soy sauce with crushed ginger and crushed garlic, she said, then you cut a chicken breast into pieces, cover the pieces with a bit of flour, fry them, and when they're all fried up, you pour the sauce over it and let it sit there awhile. Sugar, too—the sauce should have sugar.

"Sugar!" I said. "Gross."

"There's sugar in a lot of food," Mariam said. "They don't tell you about it, but there's sugar everywhere. That's how I got so fat."

"You're not so fat," my mom said. "Eat."

We bowed our heads over our plates like praying people and ate. The meatballs tasted delicious. Suddenly my mom put down her fork and said, "But you know what I think? I think one of those Filipino boys put that gun there. Don't you think, Dolly?"

I pictured Ali and his friends standing on the street corner across from our middle school's campus, smoking cigarettes and stomping the butts with their heels. You had to go there to smoke; it was outside of the school's jurisdiction, so the principal couldn't do anything about it. Ali was the only one in that group who wasn't Filipino. Once in a while, one of the boys would drop to the sidewalk and break-dance and the others would form a circle and clap and shout. They looked hot. Big shoulders. Big shins.

"Don't be racist," I said. "God!"

I HAD seen it happen. One morning after second period, Linda Tsang opened her locker and found a bullet on top of her pencil case. She screamed. Someone went to get Rod, the campus policeman. He found a gap in the roof of her locker where it had detached from the back wall, and when he opened the locker above with his master key, he found a sheaf of unopened ruled paper, a pack of cigarettes, a blackened banana peel, a loaded gun, and a handful of bullets. There was a Fugazi poster on the inside of the door, and a little mirror with a black silhouette of a break-dancer stickered to it. Oh God. I wanted to die.

"Whose locker is this?" Rod said to those of us who had gathered around to watch. "Huh? Whose locker?"

Nobody told him, but we all knew it was Ali Akhtar's locker. That afternoon, he got kicked out of school, and Mariam sent him to stay with his aunt and uncle. "I can't even look at you," Mariam told him when he got into his uncle's car. "Go, go, you're not my son." I couldn't tell how Ali felt. His face didn't change when he sat in the car. He stared straight ahead, unsmiling, as the car pulled onto the street. Mariam was the one who cried.

Even our neighbor M. Piotrowski got involved. He was the substitute French teacher at our school. The real French teacher was on maternity leave, so we were usually stuck with M. Piotrowski. He wasn't smart. He used to teach French in his living room to make extra cash. I had no idea how he had learned French in the first place but didn't want to ask him; I didn't want other kids to think we had a relationship outside of school. Back when he used to teach in his living room, Ava and Bonita had been his only students at first. Then, Mariam convinced my mom that the two of them should sign up, too.

It was my mom and Mariam who got our school to let M. Piotrowski substitute-teach when our regular teacher went on leave. In class after the gun incident, M. Piotrowski told us about the violent poem Ali had written for French I, about a boy who goes on a shooting spree in the épicerie. "I should have suspected," M. Piotrowski said after the gun incident, as if he had some special understanding of Ali from being his neighbor.

But everyone claimed some special understanding. Ali's ex-girlfriend, Lala Freeman, told people Ali had suicidal tendencies, and that phrase was rippling through the halls the way that discovered language rippled through our school all the time—gaydar, wack, Djibouti. Somebody else claimed that Ali belonged to the Trenchcoat Mafia. That he was an honorary out-of-state member.

I never said a word about Ali, though I lived next door to him. I kept my mouth shut and felt noble. I imagined being tortured—I had recently seen my first James Bond film—and still remaining silent. My eyebrows singed off with a lighter, et cetera, and I, unmoved. Ali visiting me in the hospital and asking why I hadn't talked. Telling him it was because I was loyal. Ali kissing each of the red, burned arcs where my eyebrows used to be and saying he loved me for it. Would I be his girlfriend?

AFTER MARIAM left, my mom stood from the table to wash the dishes. She thrust her hands into the sink and scrubbed the dishes vigorously, soap suds foaming at the crooks of her elbows. I felt bad for calling her racist. I watched her to see if she seemed sad. "That was your first Halloween living here," she said, nodding her head toward a photo on the fridge, taken in the courtyard. The photo was of me and Ali and another child. We were all dressed identically as clowns, with our arms around each other. It was right after Mariam had convinced my mom to move into the building. "We didn't have other friends. We invited this lady to go trick-or-treating with us. She had a son." She had remembered this aloud many times before. She was a fountain of remembrance. I didn't care about the third child or his mother. Suddenly she raised her arms out of the water and turned to me. "How can I be racist?" she said. "I'm Indian."

"Only white people can be racist?"

"Don't you think so?"

"No!"

"Well, I wasn't being racist," she said. "I only wanted Mariam to feel better. This isn't a safe place to grow up."

I didn't agree about safety. We lived on the twelfth floor of our building, a big brick box that loomed over the freeway. I loved the living room view of the traffic sliding along, red lights on one side, white lights on the other. I loved the thrum of life all around me—the cooking, the fighting, the vacuuming, the sex, the dogs barking, the babies mewling, the humming of every refrigerator, the buzzing of every doorbell, the scraping of every chair from every table· All of it came right through everyone's open doors and made me feel alive and at home.

Was it safe to leave Ava with her door open? My mom believed it wasn't. There had been robberies in the building. Everyone knew Ava was old, and not everyone was as nice as us. Some people would take advantage of her, my mom said. Mariam disagreed with my mom's reasoning. With Ava's door open, we would hear if she fell or got hurt. We would hear her ring her little bell. M. Piotrowski had his own theory, which was that, if Ava closed her door, she might start opening her windows again, which would be good for her, because it would bring ventilation into the apartment. Bonita said this was all irrelevant. What mattered was what Ava wanted, she said, and it had nothing to do with us.

AVA HAD been there the longest of anyone—forty years, according to her daughter. She was a retired seamstress, and, before she got old, she used to make handmade doilies at Christmas for everyone in the building. I remember her coming down the halls with her basket of doilies. "Doilies, everyone. Time for doilies." These days, she mostly kept to herself. But one evening, she clutched my arm as I set her plate on the coffee table. It was as if she were scared. She held me tight, so I couldn't get out of her grip. "Dolly," she said. "You've heard of Carl Sandburg, haven't you?"

"Ava!" I said. "Stop!"

She let me go. "I once visited the town Carl Sandburg was from," she said. "That was when I was living in Illinois. After he died, he and his wife were cremated! That surprised me."

"Well, what's wrong with cremation?" I said.

"It means you're cheap!" she said. "It's the easy way out!" Ava swayed and pressed her eyes shut and opened them again. "Do you know I already have my headstone picked out? My husband and me—we have matching ones. Sit down."

I sat.

She told me that the bitterest fact of her life was that her husband had inherited the biggest garbage truck company in the state and, within weeks of marrying her, gambled it all away on poker night. "Then he moved to Reno with one of those redheads. We didn't have any children yet, and I was still young, so I thought, Oh, well, here we go, and I went out dancing at the same place where I met him. That's how I met Frankie. Frankie was mean. When Frankie died, I was too old to go dancing and meet someone, so I just married Billy, because we were already friends. And I knew, because he was a nurse, that he would be kind. Male nurses are all right. My father used to say that. Male nurses are all right."

"What was your father?"

Ava said her father had been a tile-layer. She said her mother sold hats on the street. "Everyone thought we were poor," she said. "Everyone was poor, but they thought we were even more poor because my mother was the only mother who worked. The truth is that she worked because she loved it. She loved hats. Before I was born, she sold a hat to a famous actress. You can find old photographs of her wearing the hat on the red carpet, and you know it's my mother's hat, because my mother had another one exactly like it that she never sold. The boy next door said once, 'You *say* that, but how do you know she didn't make that hat after she saw the actress wearing it?' So I asked my mother, and she laughed and said, 'Well, maybe I did. Maybe that's just what I did. But, no, I didn't.' My father laid tile for the Los Angeles City Hall, too, and there's a plaque in City Hall with his name on it, saying he built City Hall. There are some other names, too, but his name is right there at the top." She glanced at the door. "Now he's coming home, and I have to clean."

"Your father?"

"My husband!"

"Which husband? What's his name?" I thought maybe I could take advantage of her dementia to get her secrets.

"His name is Ali," she said.

MARIAM LAUGHED when I told her about this. She knew Ava found Ali handsome; Ava had told Mariam many times. I also told Mariam the part about Ava's parents, and Mariam said it wasn't true. Ava's father had been a shipyard worker, Mariam said, and her mother had sewn men's pants.

"How could she make that up?" I said. "Out of thin air?"

"Who knows how people come up with stories?" Mariam said. "Maybe she got it from one of her friends. Maybe she thinks it's true."

I'd never seen Mariam's apartment because her husband didn't let her invite people over, but I knew that Ali's bedroom was on the other side of my bedroom wall. Before Mariam sent him to his aunt and uncle, I used to hear him moving around at night when I got into bed. If it was early, I could hear the death-metal background of his video game. "Fuck you!" he would shout over the music. "You're about to die, you worthless fuck!" And then, "*Bam*, you zombie *fuck*!" and the sound of guts splattering. I couldn't ever sleep. Sometimes I stayed up all night. When it

got late and the traffic became quiet, I could even hear the rustle of Ali's sheets and his snores, which sounded like a car that
wouldn't start. I felt so close to him, we might have been brother
and sister. Sometimes, when I couldn't hear him, I would cough
or bump up against the wall—to try to wake him up, to try to
make contact. I imagined that he listened for my sounds, too.
Once, after I coughed, he coughed a couple of seconds later, as
if in response. That was about as much as I interacted with Ali.
In the hallway—both in the apartment and at school—I looked at
the ground when he passed.

Now that Ali was gone, I spent the nights listening to Bonita
and her boyfriend having sex upstairs. I pressed myself to the wall
with my hand between my thighs and pretended Ali was on the
other side with his own hands down his own pants. You never
knew what you'd hear with Bonita and Alexi. Late one night, I
woke to the sound of Alexi wailing: "You stepped on my balls!
Why are you crying? You step on my dick and my balls, and *you*
start crying?"

"I'm sorry."

"I can't live without you. I tell everybody about my beautiful
girlfriend. And then you step on my balls!"

ON THE weekends, when the weather was nice, Bonita sunbathed
in the measly yellowed-grass yard between the building and the
parking lot. One morning, when I looked out our window, she
called up to me. "Come down and get some sun, Dolly." She was
sitting on a towel. Her blind mother was visiting, and the mother
sat on a kitchen chair that Bonita had taken down on the elevator and dragged outside. The blind mother had glass eyes. She
usually lived with her other daughter but sometimes came to stay

with Bonita for a few days. Bonita felt competitive with her sister, and during these visits, she spent the whole time cooking Filipino food for her mother. The mother didn't speak much English and understood only if you used simple words.

I went down and asked Bonita about the night I heard Alexi shout at her for stepping on his balls. She cried out, "I don't know, man! I came home, I was walking around, I guess I stepped on his balls! At least I'm working—that makes one of us." And she leaned back and stretched so hard that she even pointed her toes. "Mmm," she said.

I sat next to her and imitated the way she stretched—legs out, toes pointed, my arms back behind me with my palms flat against the ground. "Don't you care if people hear him screaming like that?" I said.

"I don't ever let rumors get to me, man, or I couldn't do the work I do."

Bonita was nineteen years old, and she seemed like a big sister sometimes. The main rumor about her was that dancing wasn't the only work she did at night. Another rumor was that Ali had been one of Bonita's clients and had gotten the gun through her and Alexi. Because she said she didn't care about rumors, I asked her about it.

"Bullshit," Bonita said.

"Sorry."

"I don't give a whoop. Ask me anything. But you've got to talk fast or my mom will understand us."

At that, her mom turned to us. What was strange about Bonita's mother was how she always turned to face you when you talked to her, as if she could see you with her glass eyes. I had really bad eyesight—I'd worn glasses since I was five—and her blindness scared me.

"Nanay, you remember Dolly," Bonita said.

"Uh-huh."

Bonita's glass-eyed mother watched as I told Bonita I missed Ali. Bonita said we had to come up with a plan to bring him home. We sat in the sun and thought. Bonita's mother kept watching us. Finally I said we should have a birthday party for Mariam—her birthday was coming up—and invite him. Bonita said, "See, I'd never think of a thing like that. That's why you're going to grow up and get out of here, and I never will. You're smart."

"I don't give a whoop about that," I said. "I like it here. I'm never going to leave."

I thought it was a noble thing to say, but Bonita just snorted. "You'll leave," she said.

"Bullshit," I said. "This is my home."

"Don't swear in front of my mom," she said. "You think if you stay here till you're old, this place will stay the same? No! People move, people die. Look at my mom—she wants to go back to her country, but if she went, nothing would be the same, it'd be a completely different country. Look at Ava. She used to be friends with everyone in this building, and everyone liked her. Now she's all alone, and people think she's horrible." She looked at her mother. "Hey, talk to my mom," she said softly. "Talk nicely. Call her 'Tita.'"

"Hi, Tita," I said.

"Hi," Bonita's mother said.

"Do you like Bonita's food?"

"Uh-huh," she said.

"The way you can tell they aren't real eyes is because they don't move as much in their holes," Bonita said. "She sometimes takes them out to clean them, right, Nanay?"

"Uh-huh," Bonita's mother said. The skin under her eyes drooped. Bonita said this was because of the weight of the glass.

Sibyls

*   *   *

IMAGINE BEING blind.

AT DINNER, I asked my mom and Mariam if they knew any tricks to help people sleep. "Give me a piece of paper," Mariam said, and I found an old envelope and handed it to her. She sat at the table and wrote on it for a long time and after a while handed the envelope back to me. "This is the prayer we used to recite every night before going to sleep. I don't know if it will work for you. You can try." On the paper, Mariam had written some words in Arabic, and, underneath them, a transliteration in English. She said it was a prayer for warding off jinns.

"How do you say it?" I said, and without taking the envelope, Mariam closed her eyes and raised her head and began to sing the words. They sounded familiar, like the lyrics of a song I had heard a long time ago. I had a daydream that Mariam was my real mother. That would make Ali my brother. And me, a pervert.

Mariam had brought over a dish of baklava. At the kitchen table, the three of us ate, and Mariam complained about her abusive husband, and my mom complained about not having a husband. Which was worse? That was the running debate between them.

"So I found a lot of Tupperwares under Ava's bed, and guess what was in them, people," Mariam said.

"What?"

"Pee. And I opened the closet and found more Tupperware filled with poop. It's been going on for a long time. God knows how long. I asked her, 'Why do you put your poop in your closet?' But she only shouted at me."

"So that's why it smells in there," I said. "Gross."

"Don't talk like that. Everyone gets old."

That reminded me: "Mariam," I said, "we're going to throw you a birthday party."

She brightened. "Yeah? Where?"

"Here in the building."

She paused and said, without smiling, "All right, but don't say my age."

But I could tell she was pleased. "What's wrong with your age?" I said.

"Forty's old," my mom said. "Do you know what you have to do when you turn forty-five?"

"What?" I said.

"Colonoscopy," she said. "Mariam, you have five more years."

"I did it," she said. "I didn't wait till forty. I went to the doctor and told her my mother had it—colon cancer—and she said, 'Go ahead, get it done now if you want.' And you know what? It was beautiful."

"No!" my mom said. "How can you say that?"

"I saw the picture," Mariam said. "It was so pink and red and beautiful. It reminded me of the first picture I ever saw of my baby inside me—the ultrasound."

"Was it Ali?" I said.

"Yes! It was!"

"Let's invite him," I said. "To the party."

My mom clicked her tongue. "That kind of language is for white people—invite him. Of course Ali will come. There's no invitation."

"Well, how will he know about it?"

"I'll call Ali's aunt and tell her."

"That's an invitation!" I said.

"Don't try to be someone you're not," my mom said. "If there's one kind of person I can't stand, it's people who aren't genuine. When people aren't genuine, it reminds me of your dad."

My face burned. "I am genuine," I said.

OF COURSE Ava wasn't the real Ava Gardner—the actress. She was born with another name, but she hated it and had changed her name when she was much younger. She explained you could give yourself a movie star's name as long as you didn't give the star a bad reputation or use the name fraudulently or look so much like the movie star or travel in such similar circles that you could be mistaken for her. I tried to get her to tell me her real name, but she never would. It was an ugly name, she said.

"Gertrude," I said.

"No."

"Esther."

"Yes."

"Esther? Really?"

"No."

"Olga. Mildred."

"No."

"Don't you want people to know your real name before you die?"

"Die! Who said anything about dying? What's wrong with you, girl?"

"It's Esther, isn't it?"

"No! Stop that. Do you know who Carl Sandburg is? I once visited the town Carl Sandburg was from," Ava said. Ever since the first time she grabbed me and asked about Carl Sandburg, she'd started letting me spend more time with her, instead of shooing me out. She sat in her armchair, and I sat close by, on the couch. "That was when I was living in Illinois. After he died, he and his wife were cremated. I was surprised that they were so cheap. Took the easy way out." She leaned in and put her hand on mine. "You've got a good ear, Doll," she said. "If you ever hear a strange sound from in here, come fast. It might mean I'm dying. Do you know I already have my headstone picked out? My husband and me, we have matching ones."

"Which husband?" I said.

"My husband—I only had the one!"

"Hey, Ava," I said. "Can I close the door and open some windows for a while?"

"Go ahead," she said.

I went to the door and moved the encyclopedia out of the way, nudging the door shut.

"Ava, do you know who Peter Andreivich Shuválov is?" I said.

"Never heard of him."

"He's in your encyclopedia," I said.

"Then read it," she said.

I picked up the book and carried it to the couch. When I opened it, dust flew out at me; I sneezed.

Shuválov, I told Ava, was a Russian diplomat in the 1800s.

"Russians," she said derisively. "What else is in there?"

"What do you want to know about?" I said. "Anything from Shuválov to 'subliminal self.'"

"Subliminal self, then."

Subliminal self: It came from the writings of F. W. H. Myers, especially his posthumous work *Human Personality and Its Survival of Bodily Death*.

"Go on."

"Myers"—I read—"conceived of the soul of man as capable of

existing independently of the body in some super-terrestrial or extra-terrene realm. He regarded our normal mental life as only a very partial expression of the capacities of the soul, so much only as can manifest itself through the human brain."

"Go on."

"He regarded the brain as still at a comparatively early stage of its evolution as an instrument through which the soul operates in the material world," I read. It was a dense passage. "Can I summarize it," I said, "or do you want me to read it all?"

Ava didn't answer—she just made a sweeping gesture with her hand, as if she wanted me to get on with it. I decided to summarize, skipping some words, carefully changing others that seemed archaic to me.

"A lot of the soul is beneath the threshold of consciousness— that's the subliminal part of the self. It's a part that's in touch with energizing forces—normally in limited quantities, but, in exceptionally favorable circumstances, in great floods, which for the time being raise the mental operations and the powers of the mind over the body to an abnormally high level. Myers's hypothesis inverts the dominant view, which sees everything that isn't normal as a symptom of weakness; the hypothesis of the subliminal self says many of these departures from normal mental life are actually uprushes of the subliminal self. And they foreshadow how our minds will evolve in the future, they give us a glimpse of the higher plane on which the mind of man will live, if further evolution of the nervous system makes it a better medium for the influx of the psychical energies which at present, owing to its imperfections, are for the most part confined to the subliminal self."

Ava had been silent as I read. It had taken me a long time, and I thought she had fallen asleep. But when I raised my eyes from the book and looked toward her, she nodded. "My God," she said. "I didn't know the encyclopedia was this good."

"Neither did I."

"It's been sitting there this whole time. We should read more of it—one entry each day."

"But do you believe what that man wrote?"

"I've *felt* it—what he describes."

"I haven't."

"I'll admit what you read surprises me, but not because I don't believe it exists."

"Why, then?"

"I didn't think men knew about it. I thought it was one of those things only women know about it, that we keep secret from them."

"What else?" I said. "What secrets?"

"They're different for everyone, but one of mine is my real name," she said. "Only my closest girlfriends knew it—none of my husbands did—but those girlfriends all died."

"Ava, come on, what *is* your name?"

"What else is in there?" she said. "I mean, other than Mr. Shuválov?"

"After Shuválov, there's Shuya," I told her. "Then Shwebo, Sialkot, Siam, Sibawaihi, Sir Robert Sibbald, Siberia, Sibi, Sibonga, Sibpur, Sibsagar, John Sibthorp. Sibylline Oracles. Sibyls."

"When we get to Sibyls," she said. "That's when I'll tell you."

WE THREW the party in the lobby of the building. There were a lot of us crowded in there. People we had never met had shown up, too, when they smelled the food. The adults all stood in little clusters gossiping. The kids tunneled under the coffee table. They ran around people's legs. Bonita was wearing black pants with a crease down the front. They looked like the pants that waitresses sometimes wore, and it occurred to me that I had never seen Bonita in pants before. M. Piotrowski paid for the cake.

My mom had asked Ali's aunt to tell Ali about the party, but he wasn't there yet. So I was the only one my age: not quite a child, not quite a grown-up. My mom was still upstairs, cooking. I stuck by Mariam's side. Then my mom came downstairs with a Tupperware, and all I could think of was Ava's poop. "Fancy meatballs," my mom said. "Your favorite."

We ate the meatballs. Still Ali didn't come. Finally, we brought the cake out anyway, and Mariam blew out the candles, and my mom and M. Piotrowski stood together by the table, cutting pieces of cake onto folded napkins. There were no forks. M. Piotrowski handed Mariam's husband a small square of cake and whispered something in his ear, and Mariam's husband gave a short laugh, then came over to Mariam with a big chunk of cake and pushed it toward her mouth. "What?" Mariam said softly, pulling away, casting her eyes downward.

"I'm feeding you."

"That's all right."

"Open your mouth," he said, thrusting the cake at her face. "Happy birthday."

Mariam closed her eyes and opened her mouth. When she opened her eyes, I could see that she was crying. We could all see. She didn't make any sounds—just sort of clenched her face while she chewed. When she finished eating, she cried, "My son!" There was frosting on her lips; it looked like she was foaming at the mouth. She made fists and hit her thighs. "Where's my son?" she said.

"It's a happy day," her husband pleaded.

Bonita covered her mouth. My mom clenched her jaw at

Mariam's husband as if this were his fault. I didn't know what to do. I had my mouth open, poised to speak, but I couldn't find any words. Maybe if we had invited him instead of just telling his aunt, I thought. Maybe he didn't realize it was an invitation.

Mariam recovered, though. She peeled a napkin from a stack on the table and unfolded it and blew her nose. My mom took the balled napkin from Mariam and threw it toward the trash can. It bounced against the wall, soundlessly, and fell on the floor. Mariam sniffled. "Okay," she said. "We need to bring a slice to Ava."

We stuffed ourselves into the elevator. Upstairs, Ava's door was propped open as usual. She sat up as usual with her blanket at her chin, but when we called to her, "Ava, cake," she didn't open her eyes. "Ava, Ava, cake, Ava, cake," and still she didn't move. I mean to say she was dead. I mean to say I had never seen a person sit so still. My mom said, "Oh, Mariam, oh no," and she pulled me to her in a way that was not comforting—it was the opposite of comforting, it was as if she were using me as a blanket to comfort herself. She pushed my face to her breast. "Stop it," I said, and I shoved her from me and looked again at Ava.

I could not stop looking at her. Dead. She was a human, a being of the highest order, so I had been told, and yet she—like a raccoon on the roadside or a fly on the windowsill—was dead. "What the hell?" I whispered. She wore her nightgown. On the table before her lay an uneaten rice cake. I mean to say we stood in the doorway, and I waited for one of the adults to act, and when none of them did, I realized they, too, were waiting for someone else to act. I mean to say that if she had rung the bell, none of us heard it. All of us eating cake while she went cold. Gone to the land of Peter Andreivich Shuválov.

After the coroner came to retrieve her body, which he zipped in a bag and placed on a long stretcher, I was ready to gather around with the neighbors and share memories of her. I had seen movies. I had a notion that we would sit together all night, maybe in our apartment, and reminisce. There would be finger food. I was all geared up. But it didn't happen. Everybody was exhausted and embarrassed. We each shuffled into our own apartments and murmured goodbyes and shut our doors. It was as if nothing had happened.

But it happened. It did. I remember it. I remember how Mariam came over after a few minutes, and when she and I sat at the kitchen table, I noticed a crust clinging to the tiny bulbed corner of her eye. I remember how my mom stood at the stove over a kettle of water and lightly tapped her foot. I remember how there stood on the table a dried yellow chrysanthemum in a mason jar that we kept there to hide the ringed stain of a coffee cup. How the whiteness of the sky pressed in through the window. How the couch's stuffing, coming out its seam, was like a bit of cloud. How the building wheezed and creaked under our weight. How alive we were. I remember it. We were here.

ACKNOWLEDGMENTS

STARTED WRITING STORIES in an introductory creative writing class at Stanford taught by Adam Johnson. His caring mentorship played a major role in my development as a writer of short stories, as did the support of the other creative writing faculty at Stanford University, especially Tobias Wolff and Daniel Orozco. At Stanford, I also met the brilliant and steadfast friends who played an even bigger role and remain at the center of my writing world. Those friends Alice Sola Kim, Anna Kerrigan, Anna North, Annie Wyman, Anthony Ha, Jenny Zhang, Karan Mahajan, Kathleen Founds, and Tony Tulathimutte—are among the first readers of most of the stories collected here.

I'm grateful to the Iowa Writers' Workshop, where I had the warmest and most collegial of experiences writing and revising short stories, including several that appear in this collection. Thanks to Charles D'Ambrosio, Edward Carey, Ethan Canin, Elizabeth McCracken, and Lan Samantha Chang for their guidance and support, as well as to Connie Brothers, Deb West, and Janice Zenisek. I appreciate all my dear friends and colleagues from graduate school, especially Gerardo Herrera and Sarah Heyward.

Acknowledgments

Others who helped with these stories include Amy Bonnafons, Andi Winnette, Colin Shepherd, Colin Winnette, Chris Lee, Daniel Levin Becker, Esmé Weijun Wang, Greg Larson, Jennifer DuBois, Mauro Javier Cardenas, Max Doty, R. O. Kwon, and Sam Forman.

The Writers' Workshop, the Canada Council for the Arts, the Jeffrey G. and Victoria J. Edwards Prize, the Rona Jaffe Foundation, MacDowell, and the Yaddo Corporation gave me crucial time and space to write this collection. I'm grateful to Michael Koch and *Epoch* for editing and publishing my first story. Stories in this collection have been shaped by the editorial guidance of Benjamin Nugent at *Assignment*, Benjamin Samuel at *Bomb*, Claire Boyle at *McSweeney's*, Colleen Hollister at the *Black Warrior Review*, Danielle Evans and Dora Malech at *The Hopkins Review*, Hannah Tinti at *One Story*, Laura Furman at *The O. Henry Prize Stories*, Linda Swanson-Davies at *Glimmer Train*, Michelle Wildgen at *Tin House*, Oscar Villalon at *Zyzzyva*, and Tyler Cabot at *The Chronicles of Now*.

Susan Golomb has been a dream as an agent and friend. I admire her creativity, in craft and in business, and appreciate her constancy. Susan's assistants past and present—Sasha Landauer, Remy Bohrer, Madeline Ticknor, Mariah Stovall, and Scott Cohen—also provided important editorial insight and support. I appreciate Writers House and everyone there, including Peggy Boulos Smith, for their long-term support of my writing career.

I couldn't be luckier that the legendary Alane Mason is my editor and that everyone at W. W. Norton, particularly Erin Lovett, Meredith McGinnis, and Mo Crist, have given me such a welcoming editorial home. The same is true of Peter Blackstock, Clare Drysdale and their colleagues at Grove Press in the

Acknowledgments

U.K. and of Rahul Soni, Udayan Mitra, Ananth Padmanabhan, and everyone at HarperCollins India.

In Colorado, Andrea Dupree, William Haywood Henderson, and the Lighthouse Writers Workshop have provided me with the most supportive creative home, as has the Colorado State University creative writing program.

Dr. Jose Fernandez-Solis responded gamely to a blind email and talked to me in great detail, over Zoom, about how one might go about building an ark.

The influence of my sister, Krishna Dweepa Vara, is present throughout this collection; the poem in "The Eighteen Girls" is written by her. Sophie Parker's influence appears throughout these pages as well, as does that of my parents, Vidyavathi Vara and Krishna Sastry Vara. I'm grateful to Dana Mauriello for her love and support. Ana Silos cheered me on in the final stretch. Gratitude to the Altschul, Graham, Mauriello, and Parker families as well.

The last and biggest acknowledgment is to Andrew Altschul for the care and partnership that made it possible for this book to exist and to Kavan Altschul for dealing admirably with having ended up with two writer parents and for hosting all the other kids at the readings.

The following stories were published in slightly different forms in the following publications: "The Irates" in *The Hopkins Review*; "I, Buffalo" in *Tin House* and *The O. Henry Prize Stories 2015*; "This Is Salvaged" in *Assignment*; "You Are Not Alone" in *Black Warrior Review*; "Unknown Unknowns" in *The Chronicles of Now*; "Puppet Master Made the Puppets" in *McSweeney's*; "The Eighteen Girls" in *Bomb*; "What Next" in *One Story*; and "Sibyls" in *Zyzzyva*.